FOUL PLAY

USA TODAY BESTSELLING AUTHOR
MICHELLE IANNARELLI

Cover Model: Randy Richards
www.facebook.com/randyrichardsmodel

Photographer: CJC Photography
www.facebook.com/CJCPhotography

Design: Dynamic Design Team
www.dynamicdesignteam.com

Editor: Out of the Blue Editing

Formatting: Champagne Book Design
champagnebookdesign.com

This book is dedicated to Monica DeSimone.

Thank you for always being my cheerleader
in good times and in bad times when I needed you the most.

Everyone needs a Monica in their life and I'm so blessed that
you are in mine.

I love you more.

xoxo

POWER PLAY
BY
MICHELLE IANNARELLI

Dare to reach out your hand into the darkness,
to pull another hand into the light.
—Amrit Desai

PROLOGUE

"Ma-Ma, I picked you some fresh flowers from the garden."

A weak, frail hand reached out to take the flowers from the smiling eight-year-old. "My sweet Tiano, you spoil your Ma-Ma." She gasped for air.

The young boy climbed up onto the bed, sat beside her and stroked her cheek. "It's ok, Ma-Ma, I'll take care of you."

She swallowed, lifted her hand up to her son's cheek and with all her might gave him a smile. "Tiano, soon it will be time for Ma-Ma to go and be with your Nona and Papa."

"I don't want you to leave me, Ma-Ma." Christiano laid across her body and hugged her.

Bella reached up her hand and patted her son's head. "I don't want to leave you but it's time for me to go."

"But…but, I will miss you so much." Tears started to roll down Christiano's cheeks.

"Tiano, promise me that you will grow big and strong."

"I promise."

"And you will marry someone you love with all your heart and soul. That you will have a family one day…and you'll tell your children about me and how much I loved you."

"What if I forget you, Ma-Ma?" Christiano lifted his head and looked at his mother.

She reached her hand under the pillow beside her and pulled out a gold chain with a locket. Inside was a photo of her and Christiano. "Keep this with you and you will never forget me."

The little hand reached out, took the locket, and kissed it. "Thank you, Ma-Ma." He leaned up and kissed his mother's cheek.

"Tiano, promise me that when you grow up you will not follow in your father's footsteps. He is a good man, but I want so much more for you, my son."

"I want to be an animal doctor."

A tear rolled down her cheek. She kissed her son for the last time. "Make me proud, Tiano, do good things, and never forget how much I love you."

"I love you too, Ma-Ma."

"My...beautiful...boy."

"Ma-Ma, you're so quiet...Ma-Ma! Ma-Ma!"

CHAPTER 1

Christiano glanced over at Lucia and smiled. "I can't believe you're going to be my wife." Christiano reached for Lucia's hand.

"Believe it." Lucia lifted Christiano's hand to her lips and kissed it. "I love you, Dr. Bucati."

"I love you too, and shall I remind you that I'm not a doctor yet."

"It's less than a week until graduation."

"I think we should celebrate by eloping."

"What about your father?"

"My father will want us to have a big wedding and invite all his friends."

"Ahh, and I thought that you were going to say that you were afraid that your father would forbid you to marry me."

Christiano pulled Lucia onto his lap. "Why would you think that?"

She shrugged. "I don't know it's just the way he looks at me sometimes. Almost like he wishes I'd disappear."

"News flash, he looks at me like that too. He's always so busy working that he never has a minute for anyone else."

Lucia could hear the sadness in Christiano's voice. She ran her hand through his thick dark hair. "I know that you've felt alone since your mother died but Chris, you're not alone anymore." Lucia kissed his lips. "You're stuck with me now."

Christiano smiled and then laid Lucia onto the bed and kissed her. "Good, because I'm going to love you forever."

"*I want him taken care of!*" Giorgio did not wait for a reply, he ended the call.

"Can I pour you a drink, Sir?"

"Yes, make it a double."

"Here you go, Sir."

"Thank you."

"What time should I tell the flight crew to have the plane ready?"

"To go where?"

"Christiano's graduation is Thursday."

"DAMN! It slipped my mind."

"Understandable, Sir, you're a busy man."

"That's no excuse. His mother would roll over in her grave if I missed his graduation."

"You must be quite proud."

"Proud? On the contrary, I raised my son to survive on his own, to be strong, and instead he decides to throw his life away and care for animals. He is weak and pathetic. He should be here learning the family business."

"But isn't he returning home after graduation?"

"That was the agreement when he left."

"Kiss for good luck." Christiano puckered up.

"You don't need luck, but I'll kiss you anyway." Lucia kissed Christiano. "When are you going to tell your father?"

"I guess when I see him."

"Maybe you should call him and tell him so that he will have time to calm down before he arrives."

"I thought about that, but he always says that business should be handled face to face."

"This isn't business this is about your happiness."

"My father considers me business."

"Sometimes I find it hard to believe you have his blood running through your veins."

"My mother was an incredible woman."

"I wish I had gotten to meet her."

Christiano smiled and then placed his hand on Lucia's cheek. "She would have loved you."

"How can you be so sure of that?"

"Because she told me all she wanted was for me to be happy, and you make me happy."

"Thank you for letting me know." Giorgio tossed his phone down onto the table with disgust.

"Is everything ok?"

"No, Daniel, everything is not ok. My son just interviewed for a partnership at a veterinary hospital."

"Oh."

"In California!"

"I'm sorry."

"He gave me his word that he would come back home after he finished school."

"That was before he met Lucia."

"I'm surprised she hasn't gotten herself pregnant to stake her claim on him."

"They may actually be in love with each other."

"She's not right for him. He needs a strong woman not some health freak who has corrupted him with protein drinks and saving the environment for every human and animal. Christiano should be drinking fine wine and feasting on beautiful women. He could be a very powerful man if he chose to follow his given path." Giorgio's phone vibrated. *"Yes. He did what? Stand by for further instruction."* He ended the call and turned to Daniel. "It seems that my son is full of surprises."

"Sir…"

"Christiano and Lucia just applied for a marriage license."

"What can I do, Sir?"

"You're dismissed."

"Excuse me?"

"Daniel, you've always been close to my son and when he comes home, he will need a loyal friend. Therefore, you cannot be a part of this."

Daniel nodded before leaving. Part of him wanted to call Christiano and warn him but he knew that would only lead to his own death.

Christiano grabbed Lucia's hand. "I can't believe that by this time tomorrow we'll be married."

"I can't wait to be your wife."

"We can start the pre-honeymoon when we get home tonight." Christiano gave Lucia a quick wink.

Lucia rubbed her hand across Christiano's thigh. "Oh, Baby!"

Christiano's phone started ringing. "Shit!"

"It's your father, aren't you going to answer?"

"I'll call him back later. He probably just wants to tell me that he's too busy to come out for my graduation."

"Well, whether he comes or not you're going to have to tell him you aren't going back home, you're buying into a partnership, and last but not least, that we are getting married!"

"You'll never come last and you certainly are not least. You're my whole world, Lucia."

Christiano turned the corner. Three big dark SUV's pulled up one on each side of him and one behind him.

"Chris, what's happening? I'm scar..."

Bullets shattered the windows before the SUV's took off. Christiano swerved and hit a parked car. Once the car stopped, he turned and looked toward Lucia. She was covered in glass and blood. "Lucia...Lucia, Baby! Answer me... Lucia...Please." He pulled her near lifeless body from her seat and held her in his arms as he sobbed.

Lucia flickered her eyes open and spoke in a whisper. "Your mother's here."

"Lucia, no don't..."

"I love...you."

Christiano was shaking. He thought back to the day that his mother had died in his arms. He looked down at his precious Lucia. "You promised you'd never leave me."

Christiano opened his eyes and for a moment he thought it was all just a terrible nightmare but then he heard the beeping of a machine and realized he was in the hospital.

A nurse came in. "Oh, you're awake."

"I want to go home."

"You're not in any condition to move at this time."

He took off the oxygen and then started yanking wires from his chest. "I don't care."

The nurse opened the door and yelled. "I need help in here!"

Christiano had managed to sit up, had one leg dangling and was pulling out the IV when a second nurse and an orderly came rushing in. "Mr. Bucati, you need to get back into bed. You just had surgery…"

"I. DON'T. CARE!" He tried to stand up and that is when his father came in.

"Son!" Giorgio pushed his way between the nurse and the orderly.

Christiano collapsed in his father's arms. "She's gone…I can't live without her. I want to die."

His father was sickened that his son was collateral damage. Someone surely would pay for that. Right now, he had to nurse his pitiful son back to health. Once he had him back home, he would make sure to school his son in revenge. Then he was certain he could make a real man out of him.

CHAPTER 2

"**H**ow is he?"

"Physically his body is healing but…"

"Emotionally he is weak." Giorgio stomped across his office. "It's been two weeks. He needs to move on."

"Yes, it has *only* been two weeks. I recall when Bella died it took you months before you were back to your old self."

"She was my wife. We had a child together."

"Give him some time to grieve. It's not like he can do much right now anyway. That bullet tore him up pretty bad."

"Yes, and those men who missed the correct target have been dealt with."

"All of them?"

"Not all of them. I had to let a few live so that I can seek them out when my son is ready to avenge his Lucia's killers."

Christiano stared blankly at the ceiling. It had been fifteen days since he had held Lucia in his arms. He couldn't believe his father was there when he needed him. He made all the arrangements for Lucia's burial and then packed up Christiano's belongings and escorted him home. It gave him slight comfort in knowing that Lucia was buried next to his mother. He felt as if she would care for her. Lucia grew up in an orphanage and never had a family. In fact, it was one of the first things that brought them together. A conversation had come up while in a study group about mothers and how selfless they are when it comes to caring for their children. Lucia comforted him when he spoke about his mother. It wasn't until he invited her out for tea that she told him how her parents, or her mother rather, abandoned her at birth. Here she was comforting him, and he was the lucky one who had a mother who loved him, he had memories, and he had a father at home who in his insane way loved him.

"Christiano, may I come in?" Daniel poked his head inside the dark room.

"I don't want to talk."

"Ok, then how about you listen?"

"Daniel, I appreciate…"

"I'm not going to lecture you about grieving."

"Ok."

"I know that you need time to heal both emotionally and physically. However, I also know that if your mother were here, she would tell you to fight to get well and she'd insist on feeding you."

"Then it's a good thing that she's not here."

"No, but I am. I have looked after you since your mother left us and it's killing me to see you in such pain. Please, Kid, let me help you."

"How? How can anyone help me?" Christiano looked at Daniel. "I want to die. I've thought day and night about ending my life."

"Then why haven't you?"

Christiano sat up. "I don't know."

"Because you don't want to let your mother down?"

"She'd be so upset with me."

"So, what now?"

"I guess I have to find a way to survive."

"This one will do."

"Good choice."

"What is it about animals?"

Rex looked up at his boss. "They're cute."

"I'd much rather see one mounted on my wall or on my dinner plate. I have no use for these annoying creatures when they're alive."

"So, why are you making this purchase?"

"For my son. He is taking much longer than I had hoped to come around. He has this distasteful love for animals, so I am purchasing him one."

"Sign this and then he is all yours."

Giorgio looked at the breeder and exhaled. "Lucky me."

Rex held back a chuckle.

Christiano was asleep when he felt something wet rubbing against his face. He opened his eyes to the most adorable little Labrador puppy. He smiled and reached his hand up to pet it. "Hey!"

"Ahh, so that is where he ran off to."

Christiano sat up and was holding the puppy in his arms. "He must know I'm a sucker for puppies. How did he get in here? Who does he belong to?"

The puppy kept licking Christiano while its tail wagged frantically. Christiano smiled. Giorgio may have let a small smile escape when he saw the glimmer of life return to his son. "He's yours."

Christiano looked at the puppy and then back at his father. "Mine?"

"I know you've been struggling as of late. I thought that perhaps this furry creature could help you."

"Father, this is the nicest thing you've ever done for me. Thank you."

"I know you think I'm heartless and uncaring, but I do love you, Son."

"I love you too, Father."

Daniel came into Christiano's room with a tray holding two plates. "If you tell your father that I had the cook prepare beef stew for two and allowed this animal to feast along with you in your bed I will deny it." Then he placed down the tray and winked.

Christiano smiled. "Thank you, Daniel."

"Whatever it takes to get you to eat, Kid."

Christiano patted his leg. "Up, Ti amo!" The puppy hopped up onto the bed. Christiano removed the lid from the smaller plate and allowed the puppy to feast. Then he lifted the lid from the other plate, grabbed a fork and began to eat. The puppy decided to stick its nose into Christiano's plate but Christiano redirected him back to his plate.

"Had I known that such a small creature could bring you such joy I would have begged your father to get you one years ago."

"I love animals. Lucia did too. The home we planned to buy was on a tremendous piece of property with acres and acres of lush green grass. We were going to have chickens, horses, cows and a few cute pups like this one here." Christiano pet Ti amo.

"You know you can still have that one day."

Christiano swallowed. "I don't think I could ever love anyone else the way I loved Lucia."

"Maybe you never will but that doesn't mean that you'll never love again."

"Father never did."

"You father was married and had a child before he lost your mother."

"Why is life so unfair, Daniel?"

"I don't know but if I could give anything to fix it for you I would. Good night."

"Good night." Christiano picked up Ti amo and hugged him. "I love you little buddy."

"Where is Christiano?"

"I suppose he is in his room, Sir."

"Rex, if he was in his room, I wouldn't be asking you!"

"I will go looking for him." Rex darted off.

Daniel entered the study. "Rex said that Christiano isn't in his room?"

"No, he is not. I've alerted security."

"Do you think someone managed to come into the house..."

"I don't know but he's gone!"

"I will search for him."

Giorgio pounded his hands down onto his desk. Where the hell was his son? He had been held up in his room for over two weeks and now he's vanished. He poured himself a drink and the front door slammed. He could hear talking. As he got to the doorway, he saw Christiano with his furry friend in tow. "SON!"

Christiano looked up. "I'm sorry, Father, I didn't mean to worry you. I took Ti amo for a walk. I didn't realize I'd been gone so long. I needed to stop and rest before walking back."

Giorgio stood there staring at his son and then down at the fur ball sprawled out at his feet. He wanted to yell at his son for wandering out and panicking him but instead he nodded. "It's good to see you outside of you room."

"Thank you, Father."

"Perhaps you will join me for lunch?"

"I'd like that."

CHAPTER 3

Christiano approached his father's door and was about to knock when he heard his father talking to Daniel.

"It's been a month already."

"I know but I don't think he's ready."

"Don't you think he has a right to know who killed her?"

"He does but I don't think he's ready to meet the men who took Lucia…"

Christiano burst through the door. "You know who killed Lucia?"

Giorgio and Daniel turned and looked at Christiano who was standing there seething like a rabid animal.

"Son, I told you I would find the men responsible for her death."

"Who? Where are they?"

"Christiano, you need to calm down." Daniel reached over and placed his hand onto Christiano's back.

Christiano pulled away. "No, I'm not calming down!"

Giorgio had all he could do to contain his excitement that his plan to suck his son into his world of power and crime was becoming a reality in front of his eyes. "I will bring you to them."

"I want them to pay for what they did."

"Daniel, call Jay and have him on standby to depart this afternoon."

The plane ride was quiet. Christiano had so much anger and emotion running through him it was difficult to concentrate long enough to carry on a conversation. Once they pulled up in front of what looked like an abandoned warehouse his father turned to him and handed him a gun. "You're going to need this, Son."

Christiano looked down at the gun and then up at his father. "I thought you said that your men had them?"

"They do."

"Then why do I need protection?"

"You don't."

"You brought me here, so I could kill them?"

"I did. Christiano, you are a Bucati. Nobody takes from us without consequence."

"I hate them but if I take their lives then I'm not any better than they are." Christiano sat back into his seat.

"So, I should just call the police and have them carted away and maybe they'll do a few years in prison while you spend the rest of your life without Lucia."

"Killing them won't bring her back."

"No, it won't, but avenging her killers and knowing that they paid for what they did will give you peace and justice for Lucia."

Christiano took the gun. "Lucia deserves justice."

Christiano was so pumped with anger from his father fueling him that by the time he stood in front of the three men, he was more than ready to kill them…or so he thought.

His father and Daniel stood behind Christiano. Giorgio

could barely contain himself. His son was finally going to become a real man.

Daniel was worried about the repercussions this would have on Christiano. He was a kind soul much like his mother. Deep down he wasn't a killer. "You ok, Kid?"

Christiano nodded and walked closer. He looked at the three who were tied to chairs. His father had his thugs standing off to the side. "Why, why did you kill her?"

The three men laughed. One dared to speak. "Who cares, it's one less bitch in the world!"

Christiano raised the gun and pulled the trigger. He hit the man between his eyes. He stumbled back after realizing what he had done.

His father growled from behind him. "AGAIN!"

It was like a dream. The men weren't even afraid to die as they smiled and taunted Christiano. All the while he kept seeing Lucia's blood covered body as she died in his arms. He raised the gun and held it up to the man's head. "I HOPE YOU ROT IN HELL!" Then he pulled the trigger, turned, and pulled it again.

Daniel took the gun from Christiano's shaking hand and handed it off to one of the thugs. "Deal with this when you dump the bodies."

Christiano stood there frozen as he stared at the three dead men. His father hugged him. "You've made me a very proud man today, Christiano."

"It's over. Lucia can rest in peace now."

His father pulled away and handed him a cigarette. "Here."

Christiano wasn't quite sure why he accepted the cigarette. He had never smoked. He was or at least had been a health freak. He let the smoke escape between his lips as he watched his father's thugs drag off the men he had killed. He wanted to feel remorse, but he couldn't. All he could feel was cold and empty.

The plane touched down, Giorgio came from the back of the plane and stopped beside Christiano. "I made reservations at Giuseppe's."

"I'm not hungry."

"Then you'll come and drink."

"I murdered three people today." Christiano shook his head.

Giorgio placed his hand firmly on his son's shoulder. "Lucia can be at peace now. You've given her the final gift of avenging her killers. Now we should break bread and celebrate her life."

"Fine, but I want to visit her grave first."

His father rolled his eyes. "I suppose we'll have a few minutes before dinner."

"Thank you, Father."

Christiano walked up to Lucia's grave and stared at her headstone for a moment before placing down the flowers he brought. "Hi, Baby, I miss you so much. It feels like a lifetime since I've held you in my arms." He wiped away his tears. "I did something today that I know was wrong, I should hate myself for it, but Lucia, I did it for you. I needed closure. It's so hard to go on without you. I wish I had died with you that day." Christiano dropped to his knees in tears.

Daniel came up behind him. "Don't say that. You have your whole life ahead of you."

Christiano stood and wiped his face. "After I killed those men, I should have turned the gun on myself." Christiano stepped around Daniel and headed back to the car.

Giorgio had a table full of food awaiting their arrival. Christiano however, headed straight for the bar. He had three shots of whiskey before grabbing the bottle and heading over to the table.

"Eat, Son!"

Christiano picked up a fork and nodded. He took a few bites and then returned to drinking. "May I have a cigarette, Father."

Giorgio looked at his son and smiled. He held up his glass and nodded to Christiano. "To my Son!"

Daniel raised his glass. "To Christiano!"

Christiano took a few more gulps of whiskey from his glass before standing. "Cigarette."

Daniel pulled a pack from his breast pocket and handed it to Christiano.

Christiano was outside smoking. It was late, he was exhausted and feeling a bit drunk. He scrolled through his phone looking at photos of Lucia.

"She's beautiful."

Christiano pocketed his phone before looking up. "She's dead."

The young woman looked mortified. "Oh, I'm so sorry."

"She was my fiancée."

"Again, I'm sorry."

"I feel so alone without her."

"Do you want to go somewhere and have a drink?" She smiled and rubbed her hand up and down his arm.

Christiano nodded. "Yeah."

"Come on, I'll make you forget how alone you feel."

Christiano woke up and looked around. He had a killer hangover. "He's alive."

He laid his arm over his face. "Really, I thought I died and went to hell."

"Here, drink this."

Christiano reached out his hand and took the mug. "What is it?"

"Just drink it."

He chugged it down. "That was disgusting!"

"Give it a few minutes and you'll forget how awful it was when you start to feel better."

"If you say so."

"I'm going to make some breakfast if you want to hang around and eat."

"I should probably get going. Thank you though and thank you again for last night. I really needed a…friend."

"I know you had a lot to drink but we were more than *just* friends."

"I was drunk, but I remember." Christiano stood up and started dressing.

"I know you're not looking for a relationship but if you're ever lonely or need a friend…call me."

Christiano leaned down and kissed her on the cheek. "You deserve better than me, Monica."

CHAPTER 4

Christiano washed his hands and straightened his tie before leaving the restroom. It had been a long day.

"Happy Anniversary!"

Christiano looked at Monica and laughed. "Anniversary?"

"Yes, it's two years today that we consummated our friendship." Monica smiled.

"Friendship is what this is called." Christiano laughed.

"We are friends, aren't we?"

"Yes, of course we're friends. Well, until Josh forbids it."

"I told Josh that you were part of the package."

"No threesomes for me?"

Monica swatted Christiano. "You're the one who practically forced me to go out with Josh."

"That's right."

"Why do you seem jealous?"

"I'm not jealous. I just don't want to lose you. I've gotten pretty used to having you around."

"You could have kept me all to yourself…"

Christiano placed his hand onto Monica's cheek. "You deserve so much better than me."

"So, you say."

"I say."

"I don't mind your buddy having dinner with us, but I'd like some time alone with you."

"He's coming back in."

"Hopefully, he has to leave."

Christiano sat. "I'm sorry but that couldn't wait."

"It's ok, it gave Monica and I some alone time."

Monica elbowed Josh. "Is everything ok?"

Christiano looked between Josh and Monica. "I should go."

"NO!" Monica grabbed Christiano's hand. "Josh wasn't exactly joking about alone time, but we haven't even had dinner yet, Chris. You can't go."

"Ok, but once dinner is over, I'm going to head out."

"Look, I didn't mean to make you feel unwelcome."

"I get it."

Monica looked between them. "Breadstick?"

"Hey, what are you doing here?"

"Having dinner. It's what people typically do at a restaurant, dear brother."

"People, but not you. You're usually held up on some case eating food out of a takeout container."

"True."

"Do you want to come sit with us at our table?" Josh tilted his head toward the table he left Monica and Christiano sitting at.

"Who's the suit?"

"Monica's friend. In fact, he's single, and you'd be doing me a huge favor if you'd come meet him."

"So, you want me to hook up with your cock blocker?" Arianna shook her head and laughed.

"No, just eat with us."

"I'm already eating."

"Please, Ari."

"Ok, but you owe me one."

"I'm sorry Josh is being a jerk."

"Hey, he just wants to make sure he gets dessert." Christiano winked.

"Oh, he'll get his dessert." Monica giggled.

"I hope you don't mind I invited my sister to join us."

Monica got up and hugged Arianna. "Come sit. It's so nice to see you again."

Christiano stared at Arianna. She wasn't the most beautiful woman he had ever seen but there was something about her that instantly intrigued him. He stood up and extended his hand. "Christiano Bucati."

Arianna looked him up and down before shaking his hand. "Arianna Ricci."

"But we call her Ari."

Christiano pulled out the chair next to him for Arianna. Arianna looked up at Christiano. "Thank you."

Christiano nodded.

The night flew by. Christiano and Arianna were still sipping espresso and talking when they noticed the wait staff standing around waiting for them to leave so that they could close.

"I think we had better get going."

Arianna put down her coffee cup. "Yeah, I think we've overstayed our welcome."

Christiano stood and pulled his wallet from his pocket. He reached inside and pulled out several hundred-dollar bills and dropped them onto the table. "This should make it worth their while."

Arianna grabbed her purse and got up. "I enjoyed talking to you."

"I did too. Can I walk you to your car?"

"I'm walking but I can walk you to your car if you'd like?" Arianna let out a giggle.

"Walking at this hour!"

"I walk at all hours."

"I'm taking you home."

"It's not necessary."

Christiano lifted her chin with his finger and looked her in the eyes. "I said, I'm taking you home."

The limo pulled up in front of Arianna's townhouse. "This is it."

Christiano opened his door and then walked around the limo to help Arianna out.

Arianna climbed out of the limo and looked up at Christiano. "Can I call you sometime?"

"I'd like that. Monica has my number."

"Monica. Shit! I don't even remember her and Josh leaving."

"I think it was during our discussion about Hawaii."

"That was early on."

"Yeah, guess Josh figured he'd make a run for it while you were entertaining his cock blocker."

Ariana laughed. "Yup!"

"Do you want me to walk you to your door?"

"I'm fine."

"Good night then." Christiano leaned down and kissed her forehead.

"Good night."

CHAPTER 5

Christiano headed into the dining room for breakfast with Ti amo following behind.

"Must that animal accompany you everywhere you go?"

Christiano smiled at Ti amo. "Apparently so."

"What is the life expectancy of one of those?" Giorgio pointed down at Ti amo.

"In our business he could very well outlive us."

"Our business is probably safer than most."

"How's that?"

"My reputation, the Bucati name speaks for itself. People fear our power. Even the authorities know we are untouchable."

Christiano knew his father spoke the truth but he also knew that one day someone would take them down.

"Did you call to collect?"

Arianna giggled. *"Not exactly but I do need Monica's phone number."*

"Why? What's up?"

"Your cock blocker is kind of sweet. He told me that if I wanted to go out sometime that Monica has his number."

"Sis, having dinner with the guy is one thing but dating him is another."

"*What is that supposed to mean?*"

"*Christiano Bucati is the son of Giorgio Bucati, the mob boss.*"

"*Don't you think I figured it out once he said his name.*"

"*Then why would you even entertain the idea of going on a date with him?*"

"*Because we had a good time last night.*"

"*You didn't let him…*"

"*NO! He kissed me goodnight…on the forehead.*"

"*Look, I don't even feel comfortable with Monica being friends with the guy.*"

"*Just because his father…*"

"*No, Ari, he has just as much blood on his hands as his father.*"

"*I'm a big girl who knows how to take care of herself.*"

"*Fine. I'll have Monica text you the dickhead's number.*" Josh ended the call.

"*Christiano Bucati.*"

Arianna looked down at the phone. His voice sounded so hard and cold.

"*HELLO!*"

"*Uh…hi, it's me, Ari. We…*"

"*Had dinner last night.*"

Arianna relaxed a little when his voice softened. "*Monica texted me your number.*"

"*So, does that mean you're willing to have dinner with me?*"

"*I'd like that.*"

"*I'll pick you up at seven.*"

28

"*Seven it is.*"

"*Ari, I look forward to seeing you.*"

"*Ditto.*" Arianna hung up the phone and smiled.

Christiano took Ti amo for a walk and when he entered the house Daniel waved him over. "I made the reservations for this evening."

"Thank you."

"Is she someone special?"

Christiano rubbed his hand over his face. "No. Lucia was special."

Daniel patted Christiano's back. "You know it's ok to move on."

"It's just dinner."

"Christiano, I never got to know Lucia but if she loved you half as much as you still love her, then I know that she wouldn't want you to mourn her for the rest of your life. She'd want you to be happy."

Christiano sat and dropped his face into his hands. "I'm afraid that if I move on that I'll start to forget her. The way she felt in my arms, her perfume, the sound of her voice when she said my name."

"She's always going to be with you. You're not going to forget her. You may spend less time thinking about her, but she'll always be right here." Daniel placed his hand over Christiano's heart.

Christiano looked up and his eyes had unshed tears. He cleared his throat. "Thank you, Daniel."

Daniel nodded. "You deserve to be happy, Kid."

Arianna spent most of her day reading article after article on the Bucati family. She wasn't afraid of Christiano or his evil father although after reading some of the accusations she should be.

Christiano seemed so kind, not anything like the monster he was made out to be. She read that he was a veterinarian and he often volunteered at the local shelter.

Once they had dinner and she told him that she worked for the district attorney he may never want to see her again. She was the enemy to a family like his.

Arianna closed her laptop and headed into her closet to look for something to wear. She should have asked Christiano where they were going so, she would know how to dress but since she didn't, she would have to make do with a black dress, scarf, and knee-high leather boots. That look would suit casual or dressy. Next, she needed a shower.

Christiano wore his typical black suit but instead of a white dress shirt he chose a red one. He didn't want to look like he was headed out for a business dinner but instead for pleasure.

Pleasure? He sat on his bed and thought back to the last time he enjoyed himself and of course it led him to his memories of Lucia. Was he capable of moving on when she haunted his every thought?

Ti amo came over and licked his hand. He looked down at the cute little lab and rubbed his head. "You know

Lucia would have loved you as much as I do." Ti amo licked him again. "Do you think she'd want me to move on?" Ti amo almost looked as if he nodded and then let out a yelp. Christiano smiled. "I hope that was a yes because I'm going on a real date tonight. It's not like the other dates I've been on. Those were just hookups for sex. Arianna is different. She likes me for me and hasn't asked about my family or money."

He stood, grabbed his wallet, and then gave Ti amo one last belly rub before heading out the door.

Christiano knocked on Arianna's door. She had the door open before he lowered his hand. "Hi!"

Christiano extended a bouquet of flowers. "These are for you."

"Thank you."

"You look beautiful."

Arianna blushed. "So, do you. Come in."

Christiano followed her around while she grabbed a vase and arranged the flowers. "You have a nice home."

"I like it. Cozy but not too small."

"Do you have any pets?"

"I wish I could, but the condo board doesn't allow pets."

"So, I take it you like animals?"

"I do, especially dogs."

"I have a Labrador. His name is Ti amo."

"Oh, what a sweet name. How old is he?"

"He's two and a half."

"Do you have pictures?"

Christiano pulled his phone from his pocket and pulled

up a picture. "Here you go." He extended the phone to Arianna.

Arianna took the phone and smiled down at Ti amo's picture. "He is adorable."

"Maybe we can take him for a walk in the park sometime?"

"I'd like that." Arianna handed Christiano back his phone.

Christiano took the phone and stared into her eyes. He caught himself as he leaned forward. No, it was too soon to kiss her. "Uh, we should go."

Arianna nodded. "Let me grab my purse."

Dinner sped by as they enjoyed lots of food, wine, and conversation. Christiano didn't even bat an eyelash when Arianna told him that she was an attorney or who her boss was. That made her feel confident in her decision to trust that Christiano wasn't as bad as all those articles claimed.

It was time for Christiano to take Arianna home, but she didn't want their date to end. She hoped that he would stay the night.

Christiano put the car in park. "I'll walk you to your door."

"I had a wonderful time tonight. Thank you."

"I did too. It's the first time in a long time that I was able to truly enjoy myself."

Arianna pulled her keys from her purse. "Would you like to come in?"

As much as Christiano didn't want the night to end

he wasn't ready yet. He knew that once he had Arianna, he would want more, and he still wasn't sure if he was capable. The last thing he wanted was to hurt her. So, he made up an excuse. "I can't. I have business to take care of before morning."

"I see. Ok." Arianna stepped back.

"Can I call you tomorrow?"

"I'd like that."

Christiano leaned over and gave Arianna a quick kiss on her lips. "Good night, Angel."

"Good night."

Christiano stepped inside and was greeted by Daniel. "Home so early?"

"I told you I was only taking her out for dinner."

"I know but I had hoped that…"

"I'm not ready yet."

"Did the date go well at least?"

Christiano couldn't help but smile. "It did."

Daniel nodded. "Will you be seeing her again?"

"I hope to."

"Maybe next time you'll want to stay for breakfast?" Daniel tapped Christiano on his shoulder.

"What if I do and then…"

"Don't go there, Christiano."

"I'm a horrible man. I don't deserve someone like her."

"We all deserve to love and be loved."

Christiano thought back to his mother and her wish for him to find love and be happy. But could he ever truly be happy? "Say I allow myself to love her, then what? Loving her means that I'm putting a target on her back. I can't lose anyone else."

"What happened to Lucia was tragic, but, Christiano, you weren't under guard and were unprepared. You have guards now and you carry weapons as well. If you have feelings for her then take the risk."

"Maybe, but I think I had better let her know what she is getting herself into beforehand."

"How do you plan to explain? It's not like you can tell her that you and your father kill people if you don't get what you want."

"I could make sure that she knows who my father is and allow her to draw her own conclusions."

"I suppose."

"If Arianna is as smart as I think she is, she'll run as far away from me as she can. Then I won't have a thing to worry about."

CHAPTER 6

Arianna sat at her desk mulling over her current case. Her mind was full of thoughts of Christiano. They had been out on five dates and each one ended with a kiss at the door. She was beginning to wonder if he was dating her for appearance sake or had a hidden agenda?

"Can I come in?"

"Sure, Leo, what's up?"

Leo closed the door and then took a seat. "It's been brought to my attention that you've been seen with Christiano Bucati and I'd like to ask why?"

Arianna stared at Leo for a moment before responding. "Yes, I've been out to dinner with him a few times over the last couple of weeks. I had no idea that I needed to obtain your permission to date."

"You are aware…"

"I am."

"Arianna, it makes no sense that someone as intelligent as…an attorney no less, would even entertain the idea of associating with that type of scum."

Arianna stood up, walked around her desk, and opened the door. "I appreciate your concern, Leo, but as you said, I am quite intelligent and capable of making my own decisions."

Leo stood up and stopped in front of Arianna. "I wouldn't have said anything if I didn't care." He raised his hand and dragged his finger down her cheek.

Arianna grabbed his finger and twisted it. "Get out!"

"Son, he can't be trusted any longer."

"Father, Malcolm has been in your employ for ten years now. Don't you think…"

"NO! He needs to be dealt with."

"Then you deal with him." Christiano turned to walk away.

His father grabbed his arm. "You don't give me orders!"

"What are you going to do…have me taken out?"

Giorgio grabbed Christiano's face and squeezed it. "Look at you, finally being a man and standing up to me."

Christiano stared into his father's eyes. "You taught me well, Father."

Christiano needed a break from his father. He thought he was going to put a bullet in his head earlier when he refused to take out Malcolm. His nerves were frazzled so he went to see the one person who could always set him back on track.

"Hey, Buddy!"

"Thank you for taking a break and meeting me."

"You sounded rattled. What's going on?"

"I had a disagreement with my father."

Monica reached out her hand and placed it on top of Christiano's. "I'm sorry."

"You know I think I freaked myself out that he was going to kill me." Christiano shook his head.

"Well, I'm happy he didn't."

"He was actually proud of me for standing up to him."

"Oh, that's good."

"Yeah. That makes twice in my life."

"Only twice?"

"He's not a very nice man." Christiano looked down at the table.

"What did you do the first time?"

"First time?"

"To make him proud?"

He leaned close to Monica and whispered. "If I tell you, I'll have to kill you."

Monica's eyes opened wide and Christiano laughed. "You jerk!"

"Gotcha!"

"I guess it's probably better I don't know."

Christiano leaned back in his seat and thought back to the day he executed Lucia's killers. "Yeah, you're right."

Arianna was disgusted with Leo. He'd been harassing her since she first took the job in the DA's office. How dare he. She threw the file she was working on into her briefcase and left. She needed some air.

She found herself at the Italian restaurant that she met Christiano at that first night. The hostess was about to seat her when she spotted Monica sitting at a table in the adjoining room. "Would it be alright if I sat with my friend?"

"Of course. I will have the server bring you over a place setting."

Arianna strolled over to Monica's table. "Hi!"

"Hey, how are you?"

"Aggravated and hungry."

"Have a seat."

Arianna looked down and realized that Monica wasn't dining alone. "Oh, I didn't mean to intrude."

"You're not intruding. So, tell me why you're aggravated?"

"There is this guy at work who took it upon himself to come into my office to warn me about Christiano but honestly, all he wanted was to cause trouble."

"But why?"

"Leo's been trying to get in my pants for years."

"What a loser."

"Exactly. He ran his finger down my cheek in a sleazy attempt to turn me on, but I showed him, I grabbed his finger and gave it a good twist. He's lucky I didn't break it."

"Why don't you report him?"

"I said something to one of the higher ups back when he started harassing me and I was made to look like the bad person. I've made it a point to avoid him if possible."

Christiano was on his way back to the table when he overheard Arianna telling Monica about her co-worker. He'd make sure to have Carlo take care of him.

"It must be my lucky day."

Arianna's face lit up. "Hi! I didn't realize it was you that Monica was having lunch with."

Christiano leaned down and dropped a kiss onto Arianna's cheek. "I needed a breather."

Monica looked between them. They were staring at one another all starry eyed. "I should get back to work."

Arianna looked down at Monica's plate. "You barely ate."

"Yeah, Monica, stay."

"Ok, if you insist."

Christiano walked Arianna to her car. "Hope you have a good afternoon."

"Do you want to come over tonight? I'd be happy to cook you dinner."

"Why cook after a long day at work, let me take you out."

"You know maybe tonight isn't good for me after all." Arianna didn't look up.

Christiano immediately knew that she was upset. "Arianna, I didn't mean to offend you."

Arianna shook her head and opened her car door. "You didn't."

"Hey, look at me."

Arianna looked up at Christiano. "I really need to go."

"You're upset and it's my fault. Talk to me?"

"Why don't you want to be alone with me?"

"I'm fairly certain we're alone now and have been on all of our dates."

"Right, but we're always out in public. Chris, are you using me?"

"WHAT! NO! Ari, I like you and I enjoy spending time with you. Why would you even think that?"

"I don't know." She shrugged.

Against his better judgement Christiano decided he would go to Arianna's home for dinner. "What time should I come for dinner? Unless you've changed your mind?"

Arianna smiled. "Seven."

"I'll be there." Christiano leaned down and gave her a kiss.

"Josh, is everything alright?"

"Yeah, why wouldn't it be?"

"You've stopped by my house maybe three times in all the time I've lived here is why."

"I want to ask Monica to marry me."

Arianna squealed as she hugged her brother. "I'm so happy for you!"

"She hasn't said yes yet. In fact, I'm kind of afraid that she won't."

"Why would you even think that?"

"I don't know. I guess I'm just scared."

"She loves you, Dummy."

"I love her too."

"Have you decided how you're going to pop the question?"

"I was thinking of asking her next week when we're on vacation. Maybe on the beach at sunset."

"That sounds beautiful."

"Thanks. So, what are you cooking?"

"Chicken Milanese with garlic parmesan risotto and roasted vegetables."

"Cooking for Christiano?"

"Yes."

"You really like him, huh?"

"I do."

Josh stood and kissed Arianna. "Watch your back."

"I always do."

CHAPTER 7

Christiano sat outside Arianna's house for ten minutes before he finally got the courage to go to the door. Life was easier feeling dead inside. Right now, he felt anxious and his stomach was in knots. He lifted his hand to knock and then decided he couldn't. He turned to walk away when he heard the door open.

"Christiano!"

Christiano plastered on a smile and spun around. "Hello!"

"Really?" Arianna tilted her head. "Looks more like good-bye to me."

"Oh, uhh…I think I left my phone in the car."

Arianna looked away. "You also didn't want to come in the first place."

Christiano walked closer to Arianna. "No, I didn't but I know how much it means to you for me to be here."

Arianna looked up and smiled. "It does mean a lot to me that you came."

"These are for you." Christiano handed her two dozen red roses and a bottle of wine.

"Thank you. Come inside."

Christiano opened the door and held it so that Arianna could enter.

Arianna placed down the wine and then grabbed a vase for the roses. "Would you mind opening the wine?" When Christiano didn't answer Arianna turned to see if he was still in the kitchen with her.

Christiano couldn't help but think about what it would have been like to have a home with Lucia. He knew that no matter how big of a house that she would have made it a home. He jumped when Arianna placed her hand on his.

"Are you ok?"

Christiano nodded. "Yes. I'm sorry. It's been a while since I've been in a *real* home."

"A real home?"

"I know that some people dream of living in a mansion but honestly I don't. It is cold and impersonal. I feel like I live in a museum. Ti amo is the only thing I have there that brings me comfort. Your home is full of comfort."

"It is quite cozy." Arianna smiled.

Christiano raised his hand and ran his thumb across Arianna's lower lip. "You light up the room when you smile."

Arianna waited a moment expecting Christiano to lean down and kiss her, but he didn't. He smiled even though he looked sad.

Christiano placed down his glass. "My God, Ari, this was one of the best meals I've had since…in a very long time."

"Ahh and you haven't even had dessert yet."

Christiano got up and picked up his and Arianna's plates. "Let me clean up."

Arianna sprung to her feet. "Oh no, you're my guest."

Christiano put down the dishes, removed his suit jacket and folded up his sleeves. "I insist." He took off his watch and turned on the water.

"That's very kind of you."

"It's the least I can do."

"I'll get the coffee started."

Christiano had hoped to have dessert at the dining room table and then leave. However, Arianna had other plans. She suggested they have coffee in the living room in front of the fire. Christiano sat there holding his coffee mug while he watched Arianna fill the fresh baked cannoli shells. "I hope you like cannoli?"

"I love it."

"Me too. Do you want yours dipped in chocolate?"

"You're killing me. I'm going to have to run twice as many miles tomorrow to work off this delicious food."

Arianna dipped the cannoli into the chocolate and then she turned to Christiano. "Open up!"

He opened his mouth and Arianna fed him the cannoli. She watched as he smiled and then closed his eyes for a moment. "My God, this is amazing."

Arianna took a bite before giving it back to Christiano. "Here you finish this one."

"Ari."

"Yes."

"Thank you."

"My pleasure."

Christiano was surprised at how relaxed he had become and at what a wonderful time he had been having with Arianna. She made everything seem so fun and easy. His life was full of complicated and hard times. Speaking of *hard*, he had better get home before he allowed himself to do something he would regret.

"I think it's time for me to head home."

Arianna laid her head against his shoulder. "But the movie isn't over yet."

"I know but I've seen it a few dozen times and I have an early meeting."

"I've only seen Star Wars seventeen times." Arianna giggled.

"Then you keep watching. I will let myself out." Christiano kissed Arianna on her forehead. "Goodnight, Angel, and thank you."

Christiano pulled the door open and Arianna reached for his wrist. "Don't go."

"I have to."

"Stay the night." Arianna lunged at him.

Before Christiano knew what was happening Arianna had her tongue down his throat. He panicked and pulled away. He didn't want to have those kinds of feelings. One kiss…one freaking kiss and his body went into overdrive and his nerves were tied in a knot. "I, I, I have to go."

"Why? Is there someone else?"

"No."

"Then why? We've had several dates. Are you not attracted to me?"

"I'm very attracted to you. Look, it's me, not you."

"That's a lame excuse for I don't like you but I'm trying to be nice."

"NO! It's the truth. Look, Ari, you deserve so much better than me."

"Shouldn't I be the one making that decision?"

"How can you? You don't know who I really am. Even I hate myself."

"I've wanted you since the first time I saw you."

"That's attraction, not knowing who I really am."

"I don't care. I know what you are capable of but, I. Don't. Care!"

Christiano pushed Arianna against the wall and kissed her. When he pulled away, he shook his head. "You should care. I'm a very dangerous man." Christiano walked out the door.

CHAPTER 8

"I thought I'd find you here." Monica smiled at Christiano who was sitting on a bench in the park with Ti amo sitting beside him.

Christiano looked up. "Hey!"

"You ok?"

Christiano shook his head. "Nope, but I somehow think you already knew that."

Monica placed her hand down on his leg and nodded. "I spoke to Josh who spent most of the night on the phone with Ari. Chris, I thought you liked her?"

"I do. That's the problem." Christiano reached down and pet Ti amo.

"Chris, you need to move on."

"I want to, I do, but I'm...afraid."

"What are you afraid of?"

"Someone hurting her." Christiano stood up and ran his hands through his hair. "Lucia is dead because of me."

Monica stood up and grabbed Christiano's hand. "That's enough! You did not kill her. Someone else killed her. You can't be responsible for other people's actions."

"I can be responsible for mine, and I am less than innocent."

"But deep down you're a good man, Chris. Don't push her away like...don't push her away."

"Monica, I never meant to hurt you."

"You did hurt me." Monica pouted. "But after I forgave you, I realized that we were meant to be friends and I like us."

Christiano leaned down and kissed Monica on the top of her head. "I like us too."

Ti amo barked and they both looked down at him. Monica knelt and pet him. "Even he agrees."

Arianna sat in her office mulling through piles of papers looking for a witness' statement. After little sleep, she was having a hard time concentrating. She was at war with herself over Christiano. Her mind told her to move on, forget about him and that she should be afraid. However, her heart and body were pushing her to hunt him down and make him hers.

"Arianna, did you find the Stewart papers yet?"

"Oh, uhh…no." She looked up at Leo who looked totally disgusted with her.

"You've been worthless since you started dating that vermin."

Arianna lunged at Leo. "GET OUT!"

Leo grabbed Arianna's wrist. "I'm not taking orders from…"

"Let go of her or I'll break your neck." Christiano spoke in a low commanding voice as he grabbed hold of Leo's arm.

Leo let go of Arianna's arm and leaned back to elbow Christiano as he shrugged him off. Christiano held on tight as he turned, twisted Leo's arm behind his back and pushed him out the door. Leo turned and looked at Christiano. "You're going to be sorry you did that. I'm not afraid of you!"

Christiano straightened his tie. "You should be."

"What's going on here?"

Arianna rushed out the door into the hallway. "Leo came

into my office, started barking at me and then he twisted my wrist. Christiano was only trying to help me."

"I want to press charges. You all saw him shove me and threaten me."

Christiano looked at the group of people gathered in the hallway. It didn't take but a glance for them to scatter and go back to their respective desks.

Arianna couldn't believe her eyes when they all retreated. Her boss, DA Manetto turned to Leo. "Go wait for me in my office." Then he turned to Arianna. "Are you alright?"

"Yes, thanks to Christiano. Leo has put his hands on me before and I reported him to DA Ryan, but he never did anything about it."

"Arianna, I will deal with him."

"Thank you." Christiano extended his hand.

"You have my word, Mr. Bucati."

Arianna walked back into her office.

Leo paced back and forth while his boss berated him for how he treated Arianna. "I can't believe that you're taking her side."

"I'm not taking anyone's side. I'm doing what's right. You know that harassment of any type is not tolerated and placing your hands on her made this matter even more serious. I honestly don't see any other choice but to ask for your resignation."

Leo let out a laugh. "You're joking, right?"

"No, I'm not."

"You're only doing this because she's screwing Bucati and you're afraid of retaliation."

"No. I'm doing my job."

"So, Bucati has you on his payroll now?"

"Look, I tried to be nice by allowing you to resign but after that comment...you're fired." He picked up his phone. "Lynn, have security come to my office at once to escort Leo Wright off the premises. He's been terminated."

He disliked Christiano before but now he hated him. How dare he threaten him in front of his pathetic co-workers who scattered in fear. Well, he was not afraid of the Bucati family, in fact, taking down the Bucati family was all he cared about now.

"May I come in?"

"Weren't you already in?"

Christiano stepped inside. "I won't apologize for throwing that jackass out of here..."

Arianna exhaled. She was aggravated and on edge. "Why are you here?"

"I wanted to talk to you about last night."

"Oh, the part where you kissed me or when you stormed out?"

"Both." Christiano sat. "I'm not a good person but I guess I'm also selfish because I can't seem to stop thinking about you."

"Christiano, what do you want from me?"

Christiano stood up. "I shouldn't have come."

Arianna got up and reached out her hand. "Wait! I'm sorry."

"Can we meet after work and talk?"

"Talk?"

"I want you to understand who I really am before..."

"I know who you are so don't think that you can scare me away."

"I won't have to try too hard." Christiano kissed Arianna on her cheek. "I'll come by after work."

"I'll be home."

"Hey, you ok?"

"Let me guess…Monica called you?"

Josh plopped down onto the chair across from Arianna and laughed. "Maybe."

"I'm fine, I guess."

"It's the guess part that worries me."

"Leo was let go. So, he is one less problem. Now all I have to worry about is what's going to happen tonight."

"Tonight?"

"Ahh, so Monica didn't spill all the beans." Arianna shook her head. "Yes, Christiano said he wants to educate me about who he is, but I think he wants to scare me away."

"Why would he go to the trouble of being honest…well as honest as someone like him…"

Ari shook her head and threw her hands up into the air. "Like him!"

"You know what his family is about. Don't tell me that he is an honest man, Ari."

"Fine. I do know. I'm not naive but there's more to him than being the son of a mafia boss."

"I want you to be happy, Sis, but I love you, and this guy frightens the fuck out of me."

"I know you do. I love you too."

"Promise me that you'll look before you leap."

"I will proceed with caution, I promise."

CHAPTER 9

Arianna opened the door. "Hey!"

Christiano glanced up briefly before entering. "Thank you for allowing me to come over."

"Come in."

Christiano walked into the dining room and sat. Arianna sat across from him. "Steve called to let me know that Leo had been properly dealt with."

Arianna looked at Christiano. "Dealt with?"

"Yes, he told me that he terminated him."

Arianna muttered. "Oh."

Christiano realized by the look of horror on her face that she thought he literally meant terminated. "Terminated as in, fired him, not killed him."

"I knew that." Arianna wasn't sure what she knew except that Christiano had a cold look about him and it was intimidating her.

Christiano opened his briefcase and pulled out some papers. "I trust you, but Daniel suggested I ask you…"

Arianna shook her head as she reached her hand up to take the papers. "Let me guess, an NDA?"

Christiano nodded. "Yes."

Arianna raised her hand. "Do you have a pen?"

"You're not going to refuse or read it first?"

"I trust you." Arianna removed the cap from the pen and signed her name before pushing the papers back across the table to Christiano.

"I…" Christiano stuffed the papers into his briefcase. "I shouldn't have come." Christiano picked up his briefcase and walked out.

Arianna waited to hear Christiano's car drive away but when it didn't, she got up and looked out the window. He was sitting in his car with his head against the steering wheel. She grabbed her sweater and headed outside.

Christiano opened his eyes when he heard Arianna knock on his window.

"Chris, come back inside."

Christiano looked up and turned off the car. He paused a moment before he opened the door. "Ari, I thought I was ready but…"

Arianna reached her hand out and placed it onto his cheek. "You can tell me anything. I've already formed my opinion of you and nothing you can say will change how I feel."

Christiano opened his briefcase, pulled out the papers that Arianna signed and tore them up. "I'm a jerk."

"Hey, what's honestly going on here?"

"I tried to fool myself into thinking that if you signed those papers that you'd be ok with anything I said because it was business. Truth is, it's not business and I care more than I should."

"Would it help any if I said I'm happy that you care?" Arianna smiled.

Christiano gave her a half smile. "Let's go inside and talk."

Arianna handed Christiano a glass of whiskey. "Maybe this will steady your nerves."

"Liquid courage." Christiano shook his head. "Who'd ever think that someone like me would need courage?"

"Chris, it's just me." Arianna placed her hand down on top of Christiano's.

Christiano gulped down his drink. "So, ummm…did you know that Steve is a Bucati family ally?"

"No." Arianna tried not to look shocked.

"You'd be surprised how many people my father has in his pocket."

"Chris, I've read stories about your father and…"

Christiano stood and began to pace. "They're not stories, they're truths. Ari, my father is a ruthless man. He wouldn't think twice about putting a bullet in my head if I crossed him."

Arianna got up and walked over to Christiano. "But you're not like him, Chris."

"I'm not a good person, Ari. I tried to escape from my father but after…" Christiano took a breath. "When I moved back home after veterinary school, I made the decision to work with my father. It's not something that I'm proud of but it's who I am."

Arianna placed her hand onto Christiano's back. "If you're not proud then change who you are."

Christiano shook his head. "You don't understand. I'm in too deep to get out."

"There's always a way, Chris."

Christiano shook his head. "No, it's too late. I've done things that are so unforgivable I can't even stand the sight of who I've become."

"Well, I welcome the sight of you." Arianna leaned over and pressed her lips against Christiano's.

Christiano closed his eyes. He waited a moment too long to reciprocate causing Arianna to pull away and step back. "Ari." Christiano grabbed her wrist, pulled her into his lap and kissed her.

Christiano pushed the bedroom door open with his foot, entered the room and gently laid Arianna onto the bed. "Last chance to run."

"I'm not going anywhere. I want you, Chris." Arianna unbuckled his belt. "Now!"

Christiano practically tore her clothes off. He'd been with so many women, but Arianna was special like Lucia. "You're so pretty, Ari." Christiano kissed Ari as he slid his fingers inside her.

Arianna reached her hand inside his pants and stroked his cock. Christiano couldn't help but moan into Arianna's mouth. "Mmm."

"Ohhh, Chris!" Arianna was so turned on that she came. Christiano sprung up, yanked his wallet from his pocket and grabbed a condom. He stepped out of his pants, removed his gun, and slipped it under the bed. "You ok, Ari?"

Arianna smiled. "I'd be better if you were inside me."

Christiano ripped open the condom, rolled it on and climbed between Arianna's legs. "I hope you never regret this."

Arianna lifted her hands to Christiano's cheeks and looked into his beautiful green eyes. "No regrets, I promise."

Christiano kissed Arianna as he slowly pushed his way inside her. "God, Ari."

Arianna ran her hand through Christiano's hair. "I've wanted you for so long."

Christiano had so many emotions running through him. He hadn't felt this way in anyone's arms since Lucia. "Mmm… me too."

Arianna dug her nails into Christiano's back and ass cheeks causing him to move faster and harder until he finally came.

Arianna waited for Christiano to come out of the bathroom. She had hoped he was just discarding the condom, but a few minutes had passed since he left the bed. Now she was afraid it was him who was having regrets. She got up and knocked on the bathroom door. "Chris, are you ok?"

Christiano splashed some water onto his face before opening the door. "I'm fine."

"Good because I was getting lonely." Arianna leaned up and kissed Christiano.

Christiano pulled away. "I need to go." He pulled on his pants.

"You were worried about *me* having regrets! You're the one who can't get away fast enough." Arianna turned and ran into the bathroom slamming the door behind her.

Christiano finished getting dressed. He thought about running out while Arianna was locked in the bathroom, but he just couldn't go knowing how upset she was. Instead he went over and knocked on the door. When she didn't answer he knocked again. Still no answer. "Ari, I'm sorry. If you want to talk, I will be outside having a smoke before I leave."

Arianna heard Christiano walk away and then her front door closed. Sadness ran through her. How could their love making be so meaningless to him? She had hoped that once they were intimate that he'd let down his guard. Maybe he wasn't ready to move forward, and she pushed him too hard?

Arianna pulled on her robe as she muttered. *"The only way to find out is to go out there and talk to him!"*

Christiano paced while he smoked not one but two cigarettes. He tried to leave after the first one but couldn't walk away. Now he was at the end of his second and Arianna still had not come outside. He drew his last drag and tossed the butt onto the ground.

"Still here I see."

Christiano swung around. "Ari, I don't have any regrets."

"Neither do I."

"You're a beautiful, intelligent woman, Ari…"

"But it's over." She turned away.

"Don't you understand that it could never work between us…you became an attorney so that you could make the world a better place by locking up criminals…not so you could sleep with them."

Arianna was furious. She smacked Christiano across the face. "Fuck you, Christiano, for making something I thought was special seem cheap, and for making me feel like a whore!"

Christiano grabbed Arianna's wrist. "You slapped me!"

Arianna looked up into his eyes. "So now what? Do you have one of your men put a bullet in my head?"

Christiano blinked a few times before belting out a laugh. He let go of Arianna's wrist and shook his head.

Arianna wasn't sure if he snapped or what.

Christiano took a step back. "You really aren't afraid of me, are you?"

"No! I'm not afraid of you or your father."

"Nobody's ever treated me...normal." Christiano shrugged. "I grew up with people feeling sorry for me because my mother died when I was a young boy. As an adult people feared me because of my father and now for the monster I've become."

"Chris, you're not a monster." Arianna placed her hand on his cheek.

"But I am."

"I see so much more when I look at you."

Christiano opened his mouth to speak and his phone rang. He pulled it from his pocket and when he saw that it was his father, he knew that he needed to answer. "I'm sorry I need to get this."

Arianna sat on the front step waiting for Christiano to finish with his call. It had been a few minutes already. Christiano swung his arm in the air and although Arianna could not hear what he was saying she knew it was loud and he didn't seem happy.

Christiano headed back up the driveway. "I'm sorry. That was my father. He needs me to take care of some business."

"You're welcome to come back later?"

Christiano kissed Arianna's forehead. "I think this is going to be an all-nighter."

"Ok." Arianna was disappointed.

"Can I call you tomorrow?"

Arianna smiled. "You better."

Christiano leaned forward and kissed her quickly on the lips. "Good night, Angel."

"Take care of yourself."

Arianna stood there watching as Christiano hopped into his Ferrari and sped off.

CHAPTER 10

Christiano sat quietly waiting outside his father's office listening while his father yelled at two of his men. He cringed at the thought that he was next. Last night had been a literal bloody mess that ended in four dead, three wounded and one man missing.

Daniel handed Christiano a glass of orange juice and some pain killers. "Take these."

"I'm fine."

"You heard what the doctor said…"

Christiano waved his hand in the air. "Yeah! Stay in bed."

"He's right. You lost a lot of blood. Kid, you could have died."

"It's what I deserve." Christiano looked down.

Daniel stepped closer. "It's not what your mother wanted for you."

Christiano grimaced as he stood up. "What she wanted was for me to live a good life, find love and be happy." Christiano shook his head. "If there is life after death then I'm certain I've broken her heart."

"Kid, it's never too late to change who you are."

"How can you say that when you know…"

Daniel placed his hand onto Christiano's chest and tapped. "Because I know that you have your mother's heart." Daniel turned and walked away.

59

After arriving at work and hearing about a drug bust gone wrong and that two of the men killed were connected to the Bucati family, Arianna was sick with worry. Which was why she was walking up Christiano's driveway. She had texted and called several times but when he never responded she decided to drive over to his house. Now, here she stood trying to get up the nerve to ring the doorbell.

Giorgio pulled his door open, took one look at Christiano and grabbed him by the elbow. "Son!"

Christiano was pale and covered in sweat. "I'm sorry, Father…"

"Christiano, what the hell are you doing out of bed?"

"I thought that you'd want to berate me for what happened last night."

"Son, you're not at fault, my men are."

"I stepped in to help but it was too late for Bunk and Ray."

"If they did their job right then they wouldn't have gotten themselves killed and you wouldn't be injured."

"I'm fine, Father."

Giorgio placed his hand onto Christiano's cheek. "Son, I don't want to lose you. Now go rest. That's an order!"

"May I help you?"

Arianna looked up at the creepy man. "I'm a friend of Christiano's."

"Is he expecting you?"

"No."

"Then I suggest you contact him and make arrangements to visit. Good day."

Arianna stepped forward. "Wait! I need to…"

"Arianna?"

"Yes!"

Daniel nodded and Rex walked off. "I'm Daniel. Christiano is in his room."

"Is he alright?"

"Why do you ask?"

"I've been texting and calling and…"

"Ahh, Christiano's phone had a mishap last night."

"Oh, so he's ok?"

"Why don't you come in and I'll bring you up to see him."

Christiano was halfway from the bathroom to the bed when his door opened. "Christiano, Arianna is here to see you."

Before Christiano got to respond Arianna pushed the door fully open and walked in. It didn't take but two seconds before she was at his side. "Oh my God, Chris, you're hurt!"

Christiano was shaking and dripping with` sweat. Daniel wrapped his arm around his waist and walked him to his bed. "I'm calling your doctor."

Christiano laid back against his pillows. "Don't!"

"I think you need a doctor, Chris."

"All I need is rest."

"Fine, but if you're not better later, I will call him!" Daniel threw his hands up in the air before storming out.

61

Arianna stood in the middle of Christiano's bedroom staring at his bruises and bandages.

"Ari, why are you here?"

Arianna realized she was gawking at Christiano. "I was worried about you."

"Why?"

Arianna walked over to his bed. "I heard that something happened last night and then when you didn't respond to my messages…"

Christiano reached for her hand. "I'm sorry I worried you."

"Daniel told me your phone had a mishap."

"It did, it saved my life."

"How?"

"Apparently, it saved me from having a knife in my heart."

Arianna's eyes grew wide. "My God, you were stabbed?"

"It's no big deal. I'm just a little weak."

"No big deal! A little weak? You're pale as a ghost, and barely made it to the bed!"

"Ari, I don't need you yelling at me."

"I'm not yelling, Chris, I'm…"

"I'll call you tomorrow." Christiano closed his eyes as he looked away.

Arianna woke to Christiano mumbling and crying out in his sleep. She looked at her watch and realized that she had been there for five hours. She had only stayed in hopes that Christiano would calm down and talk to her. He had fallen asleep without a word and so did she.

"Lu…Lu…Lucia…I love you…love you…Lucia… Lucia…I…"

Daniel came in. "How's he doing?"

Arianna stood up. Her heart was breaking. She thought she meant something to Christiano yet all he did was mumble on and on about Lucia. "I have to go." She grabbed her purse and tore out of there.

Josh opened his door expecting to see Monica but instead it was his sister. Arianna had tears running down her cheeks and a handful of crumpled tissues. "Ari, what's wrong?"

"Chris…"

"What did he do to you? Did he hurt you? I'll fucking kill him!"

Arianna grabbed Josh's arm. "Josh, he didn't touch me."

"Then why are you crying?"

"There's someone else."

"Someone else?"

"He was talking in his sleep and he said he loved her."

Josh hugged Arianna. "I'm sorry, Sis."

Arianna pulled away, walked over to the couch, and plopped down. "It's my fault. Everyone warned me and I chose to ignore them."

"You know sometimes we can't help how we feel, even if the guy is a jerk."

"I really thought he cared about me, Josh."

"Maybe he does."

Arianna glared at her brother. "You're joking, right?"

"Look, I don't like the guy but even I've had more than one girlfriend at a time."

"Lucia isn't just a girlfriend…he said he loved her."

Josh sat next to his sister and wrapped his arm around her. "Did you and Christiano discuss being exclusive?"

Arianna pulled away. "Now you're taking his side?"

"No! Not at all. I don't like seeing you like this, so I guess maybe I was trying to play devil's advocate."

Arianna leaned over and kissed her brother on the cheek. "Thank you."

"Josh, you here? Sorry I'm late."

Josh came out of the bedroom. "Hey, Baby!"

"I thought maybe you gave up and left without me."

Josh hugged Monica and then kissed her. "Not a chance I'd leave without you."

Monica ran her hand down Josh's chest. "I thought you were wearing your new shirt?"

"I was until my sister showed up and left it covered in tear stains."

Monica looked up at Josh. "Oh no, what happened? Is she ok?"

"No, it seems that your buddy, Christiano, broke her heart."

"How?"

"He apparently has another girlfriend."

"Chris? No way, he hasn't spent more than one night with the same woman…the whole time I've known him. He's not that kind of guy. Plus, I know how much he cares for Ari."

"Well, he professed his love for Lucia and…"

Monica's eyes opened wide. "Lucia? She's…Lucia was killed years ago."

Josh tilted his head before shaking it. "I guess he's still hung up on her then."

"Josh, I don't understand why Chris would even tell her that. It makes no sense. He never wants to talk about Lucia."

"He didn't exactly discuss it; he was talking in his sleep."

Monica rolled her eyes. "Oh, God, I need to speak to Chris."

Christiano woke up to find Daniel pacing in his room. "How are you feeling, Kid?"

"Still wondering why Bunk and Ray died and I didn't."

"Will you stop saying that!"

Christiano rolled over and grimaced in pain. "Least if I was dead, I'd be with Lucia again."

"I know she's been on your mind but…"

"What do you mean?"

"You were talking in your sleep. In fact, I think Arianna may have heard some of what you said because she was quite upset when she left."

"I wasn't very nice to her. I told her I'd call her tomorrow and went to sleep."

"Yes, well she was here for hours sitting with you before she left."

Christiano closed his eyes. "Dammit!"

"I'm sure once you explain she will understand."

Christiano looked away. "She's better off if I don't.

CHAPTER 11

"May I come in?"

Arianna looked up at Daniel. "Is Christiano alright?"

"Yes."

"Then why are you here?"

"I'd like to speak to you about Christiano."

"Unless it's regarding a legal matter, there isn't anything to discuss."

"Arianna, I know you care about him."

"I did but…"

Daniel walked inside Arianna's office and closed the door. "You still do, or you wouldn't have grown pale with worry when you saw me in your doorway."

"Daniel, I appreciate whatever it is you are trying to do but even if I do care, he's in love with someone else."

"Lucia is his past, you're his future."

"Then why hasn't he called me? It's been four days."

"To be honest, he said you are better off without him."

"Maybe he's right."

"If you honestly believe that then I'm sorry I've wasted your time." Daniel was out the door before Arianna could respond.

Christiano looked at Monica's face flashing on his phone. She had been calling and texting him for days. Aside from his one reply that he was in bed sick, he had been ignoring her...and everyone else for that matter. The call went to voicemail and then he got a text.

Monica: *"STOP SENDING MY CALLS TO VOICEMAIL, CHRIS!"*

Christiano grunted and then dialed Monica.

"Ahh, you were avoiding my calls!"

"Monica, can't a guy be sick?"

"Sure, if he is actually sick."

"What makes you think I'm not?"

"Have you forgotten that Arianna is Josh's sister?"

"No."

"Chris..."

"I don't want to discuss it."

"She's miserable, Chris."

"I thought that you were my friend?"

"I am your friend. Chris, talk to her. She'll forgive you once you explain."

"She's better off without me and so are you." Christiano ended the call.

Arianna couldn't concentrate so she decided to go for a walk and grab some coffee. She reached for her coffee and Josh grabbed it. "Thanks for the coffee, Sis."

Arianna rolled her eyes. "Anytime."

Josh smiled at the server and then pointed at his cup. "Can you make one more, please."

"So, what brings you out of your office in the middle of the workday?"

"I had a long boring meeting with a client and was in desperate need of some caffeine. What are you doing here?"

"I needed to clear my head, so I decided to go for a walk."

"Clear you head, huh?"

"Yeah, work stuff, you know."

Josh grabbed the second coffee and handed it to Arianna. "What I know is that jerk broke your heart and…"

"Josh, I'm over him."

"Ari, you can't lie to me."

"Fine. It's been four days since I walked out and not a word from him. So, whether I want it to be over or not…it is."

"Son, sit down."

Christiano leaned against the door frame. "I'll stand."

Giorgio shrugged. "It seems that we have a mole."

"Are you sure?"

"I'm certain."

Christiano exhaled. "Who is it?"

"I was hoping you could shed some light on that?" Giorgio studied his son's face.

"Don't you think that if I had a clue that we had a rat that I would have dealt with it immediately?"

"I don't know…would you have?"

Christiano glared at his father. "Father, are you accusing me?"

"No, not you…"

Christiano walked closer. "What are you implying?"

Giorgio stood and looked Christiano in the eye. "That lawyer you're screwing…"

Christiano's eyes narrowed and he growled. "How dare you accuse Arianna!"

"Son, I know you want to believe that she cares for you but I'm afraid she may have her own agenda."

Christiano didn't need but a moment to know that his father was wrong about Arianna. When he held her in his arms, he knew her feelings were genuine. "You're wrong. She genuinely cared about me."

"Cared? So, you're no longer lovers...interesting?"

"I know what you're thinking but I pushed her away."

"You pushed her away or did she take off once she got the information she came for?"

Christiano spun around and punched the wall. "She took off after hearing me say that I loved Lucia." Christiano exhaled before turning back toward his father. "I hurt her, and she left me. Satisfied!" Christiano walked out of his father's office.

Monica knocked on Arianna's car window. "Hey!"

Arianna hit the button and lowered the window. "Hi."

"Do you have time to talk?"

"Get in."

"I'm worried about Chris."

"Why, what's going on?"

"We had a fight...or at least it seemed that way. We've been friends for years now and he wants to just end our friendship."

"WHAT!"

"He said we are both better off without him and then he hung up on me."

"I know he doesn't want me around because he loves someone else, but you, you're his best friend."

"I told you to forget about her. He will never be with Lucia."

"I don't want to be second choice."

Monica placed her hand on Arianna's cheek. "Oh, Ari, you'd never be his second choice; you're his second chance."

Christiano grimaced in pain as he leaned down to pet Ti amo. "Ugh! Hey, Buddy, how was that bone? Huh, Boy?"

Ti amo barked before licking Christiano's cheek.

Christiano sat. Ti amo nuzzled his head against Christiano's chest. "You miss her too, don't you?"

It was as if Ti amo really understood him. He let out a soft whimper. "Mmhmm."

"You could go talk to her."

Christiano looked up at Daniel. "It's complicated...I'm complicated."

"Kid, I've had three wives and I never looked at any of them, the way you look at her."

"She takes my breathe away. I never thought anyone else could ever do that...again."

"Go find her. Talk to her about Lucia. Then tell her how you feel about her."

"My father thinks that Arianna is a rat."

Daniel looked away. "So, he said."

"Do you think she is?"

"Anything is possible, Kid, but my gut says no."

Christiano smiled. "Mine too, but my father tried to tell me she's clouded my judgement."

"Kid, the only thing that lovely lady is responsible for is that smile on your face when you say her name." Daniel ruffled Christiano's hair. "Now go!"

CHAPTER 12

Christiano drove around the block three times before he finally parked in front of Arianna's townhouse. He thought about what both, Monica and Daniel had said. He also knew that once he apologized to Arianna that he owed Monica an apology as well.

He took his time walking to the door as he thought about what he'd say or if she would even allow him to speak at all. Once he reached the door, he quickly rang the doorbell so that if his nerves got the best of him, he wouldn't have time to get away.

Arianna stood looking through the peep hole at Christiano. She contemplated not opening the door but deep down she wanted to see him. Maybe Monica was right, and Lucia was in his past. She closed her eyes, exhaled, and opened the door.

Christiano stood there staring at Arianna. "Did you come to stare at me, or do you have something to say?"

Christiano blinked. "No. I mean, yes. I want to apologize and explain if you will allow me?"

Arianna stepped back. "Come in." She closed her eyes and inhaled his scent as he passed her by. He always smelled so good. It was a mix of grapefruit and leather.

Once he was inside, he turned toward Arianna. "The last time we spoke I wasn't myself and I was quite rude. Daniel told me that you stayed to watch over me while I was asleep, and I said some things that upset you. For that, I am truly sorry."

"Sorry that I heard them?" Arianna sat on the couch.

Christiano wasn't sure where to start. He too sat and reached for Arianna's hand. She reluctantly allowed him to hold it. "I am sorry that you heard them because I know how much it hurt you. My past isn't something that I talk about because it's too painful, but I owe you an explanation."

"Do you love her?"

Christiano looked down at the floor. "Honestly, I think part of me will always love..."

Arianna stood. "You should go." Then she walked down the hall to her bedroom.

Arianna flung herself across her bed. Tears rolled down her cheeks. Hearing Christiano babble that he loved Lucia in his sleep was hurtful enough but now he was wide awake and still professing his undying love for her.

Christiano knocked. "Ari, can I come in?"

"No."

"Please let me come in. I need to explain."

"Why? What does it matter if you're in love with someone else?"

Christiano leaned against the wall. "Ari, I came here because I want to be with YOU!"

Arianna pulled the door open. "Why?"

"Because I care deeply about you and I think you care about me too." Christiano ran his fingers down her cheek and lifted her chin.

Arianna looked into his eyes. "I do but…" Christiano grimaced in pain which caused Arianna to stop mid-sentence. "Are you alright?"

"I didn't take my pain medication today. I wanted to have a clear head when we spoke."

"Come sit."

Christiano sat. Arianna sat next to him and rubbed his back to ease the pain. "I want to tell you, but I need you to know that it is *very* difficult for me to share my private life with anyone…especially this."

"Ok."

Christiano held onto Arianna's hand. He tried to find something across the room to focus on so that he wouldn't fall apart. "I led quite a boring life once my mother died. My father totally ignored me. If it weren't for Daniel I would have been completely alone. I couldn't wait to be out of the house. I was lonely and full of anxiety when I left for college, but I soon made friends. Lucia was one of them and before long we began dating. By the time I had graduated college I knew we were meant to be together. I applied for vet school in hopes of being accepted nearby so that I could stay in California with her. A few months before graduation I asked her to marry me. I planned to join another friend and become partners in his veterinarian practice. Everything was perfect. We found some houses…"

Arianna was having mixed emotions…she was hurt, jealous and now becoming angry that he was sharing this with her. She pulled her hand away and jumped up so quickly that she didn't even notice the tears rolling down Christiano's cheeks. "Don't you think it hurt me enough to hear you professing your love for her, but now you have to tell me your perfect love story!"

Christiano sat there blinking away tears. "I told how you hard this was for me. I…" He stood and it was then that Arianna saw his tears.

"You're crying?"

Christiano was on the edge. He felt so broken. He walked out.

Arianna felt guilt wash over her. He told her how hard it was for him, and she allowed her feelings to surface. She ran after him.

"Chris, wait! Please!"

Christiano stopped but he didn't turn around. "I shouldn't have come. It was never my intention to hurt you and yet, I keep doing it."

Arianna darted in front of Christiano before he could take another step. "No, it's my fault, I'm sorry. Between the hurt and jealousy…"

"You have no reason to be jealous." Christiano felt humiliated that he was such a mess. He looked everywhere except at Arianna.

"No? It wouldn't bother you if I were in love with someone else?"

"Not if they were…dead."

Arianna's eyes opened wide and then they too filled with

tears. Her heart broke for Christiano. "Oh, God, Chris, I'm so sorry. You must think that I'm the most insensitive person on the planet." Arianna wrapped her arms around Christiano. "Will you forgive me?"

Christiano woke up in the fetal position with his head on Arianna's lap. He tilted his head up. Arianna was smiling down at him. "I can't believe I fell asleep."

"I think that pain killer called bourbon may have had something to do with it."

"It may also be the reason I have this awful headache."

"Why don't I go make us some breakfast?"

"Breakfast? What time is it?"

"Five."

"SHIT!" Christiano sat up and groaned. "My father…"

"He knows where you are."

"You called him?"

"No, but there has been a car outside with two men in it for hours now."

Christiano went over to the window and peeked out. "You're right they're our men."

Arianna wrapped her arms around Christiano and rested her cheek against his back. "Thank you for letting me in."

Christiano gently turned in her arms. "Thank you for allowing me."

Arianna leaned up and kissed him.

Christiano texted Daniel while Arianna was making breakfast. He didn't want to alarm her, but those men outside were not his father's. His father's men would never allow their target to see them. Now, if only he knew who sent them, and if it were him or Arianna that they were watching.

Christiano: Daniel, quietly send some men to my location.

Daniel: What's going on?

Christiano: When I woke up Arianna told me that there were two men in a car parked outside for several hours. She assumed they were ours. I allowed her to believe they were, but they are not.

Daniel: I've shared your location with Jared and Lou. I explained to keep things quiet.

Christiano: I also need for you to arrange to have a security detail set up for Arianna. I will not allow anything to happen to her.

Daniel: Shall I have them let you know when they arrive so you can introduce them?

Christiano: NO! I do not want Arianna to know she is being guarded…at least for now.

Daniel: Understood.

Christiano: I will be here until I hear word that security is in place.

"Chris, your eggs are ready!"

Christiano pocketed his phone and headed to the kitchen.

Arianna plated the food and placed their plates onto the table.

Christiano came strolling in. "It smells delicious."

"I thought maybe you fell back to sleep."

"Nope, just going through some messages from yesterday."

"Chris, what do you do at work? I mean besides the obvious."

Christiano put down his fork. "The obvious?"

Arianna squirmed in her chair. She barely spoke above a whisper. "The killing and illegal…"

Christiano busted out laughing. "I'm sorry. It just sounded so blasé the way you asked. It also feels kind of strange to be speaking about it to you of all people who could put me away for life."

"Why don't we change the subject."

"Aside from the family hotel business I spend as much time as I can volunteering at the animal shelter."

"Why don't you open your own business? You have enough money."

"The shelter will take whatever help they can get. They're not going to judge me. But how many people want to bring their pet to see the local mafia boss' son?"

"I would…if I had a pet." Arianna smiled.

"Well, thank you. Besides dogs, what other animals do you like?"

"Actually, I love all animals. Up until I was about fifteen, I asked my parents each Christmas for a horse. Maybe I'll have pets one day when I have my own house and a family."

"What were you going to name your horse?"

"Cinnamon."

"Have you ever ridden a horse?"

"Yes, every year when I went to sleepaway camp. Camp was on a ranch and they let us ride the horses and brush them as much as we wanted."

"Horses are beautiful animals. Maybe we can go riding some time?"

"Do you own horses?"

"No, but I know some people who do." Christiano smiled.

"I'd love that."

"Then it's a date."

CHAPTER 13

"You should be more comfortable now that the stitches have been removed but I do not want you doing anything strenuous for another week. Your insides need to finish healing. Do I need to remind you just how lucky you were!"

"No, I know. I promise and I will behave, Doctor."

"Ahh, so how is my son?"

"Give it another week and he will be back to his old self."

Giorgio patted the doctor on the shoulder. "Thank you, Doctor."

"You are quite welcome."

Christiano was surprised to see his father sitting in his room when he came out of the bathroom. "Father, I thought you walked Dr. Danna out."

"No, Daniel will take care of him. We need to speak."

"Ok." Christiano sat on the bed.

"It's about the men from the car. They were working for Hugo Alvarez. Seems that he owed a favor to someone named Raul."

"They didn't get Raul's last name?"

"They claimed that was all they knew. So, Jared put a bullet in one of them hoping to scare it out of the other but after a few hours he gave up and disposed of him too."

"So, we still don't know if they were there for me or Arianna?"

"I would assume if they were Alvarez's men that it was you, they were told to watch."

"Good, because I couldn't handle losing Arianna."

Giorgio rolled his eyes. He didn't like anyone who made his son weak.

Arianna opened her office door to find a large vase of lilies on her desk. A huge smile spread across her face as she inhaled the beautiful fragrance.

"Looks like someone has a thing for you." Lynn smiled.

Arianna turned toward Lynn. "They're beautiful, aren't they?"

"Yes, they are. Odd, I would have pegged Mr. Bucati as a man who only sent long stemmed red roses."

"He does fit the bill; however, these are the most exquisite lilies I've ever seen."

"I think you had better call that man and thank him."

"I will." Arianna sat, reached for her phone, and realized there was a card between the lilies. She opened the envelope and pulled out the card. She was a bit disappointed that all it said was 'Thank You'. Then she reminded herself that she had made progress last night, and soon enough his walls would start to crumble. Arianna smiled and picked up the phone.

"Bucati."

"I'm calling to thank you for the lilies. They are gorgeous, not like any I've ever seen, and they are so fragrant."

Christiano smiled. "I'm very happy to hear that. I had them flown in from Italy."

"Italy?"

"We have many properties there with extensive gardens and some vineyards."

"So, my next surprise might be a bottle of your very own wine?"

Christiano chuckled. "Possibly. Tell me do you prefer red or white?"

"I was teasing."

"I know but these are things a man should know?"

"White is my go-to but if I've had a bad day then I don't discriminate." Arianna giggled.

"Good to know."

"Will I see you later?"

"I have something I need to take care of for my father."

"Oh, I'll let you go."

"If I return early enough, I'll text you to see if you're awake."

"Ok. Be careful."

"I will."

Christiano pocketed his phone, picked up his gun and was out the door.

Christiano's men kicked in Hugo Alvarez's door. He pulled his gun but before he could shoot, Christiano stepped inside. "Who is Raul to you?"

Hugo stood with his gun pointed at Christiano. "Get out or I will blow your head off!"

Christiano took a step closer. "You have two seconds to answer or you will end up like your men!"

Christiano's men walked forward, one grabbed the gun from Hugo's hand and the other shoved him down into his chair. "My men told you about Raul?"

"They did."

Hugo shrugged his shoulders. "Then they got what they deserved."

Christiano placed his gun against Hugo's head. "Any last words?"

Arianna pulled the door open hoping it was Christiano but instead it was Josh. "Hey!"

Josh walked in. "Don't look so excited to see me."

"I thought it was Christiano at the door."

"Ari..."

"I know what you're going to say, and I appreciate you being concerned..."

"Concerned! No, I'm downright afraid for you."

"I didn't walk into this blindly. I am very aware of what his family is capable of."

Josh kissed Arianna on her forehead. "I love you. I don't know what I'd do without you."

"Josh, Chris won't let anything happen to me."

"Monica always says the same thing but how can you trust someone like him?"

"I don't know, we just do."

Daniel was bringing Ti amo in from his walk when he noticed a shadow in the garden. He opened the door, put Ti amo inside and then slowly approached the garden. Daniel reached for his gun, took one step into the garden, and immediately knew that it was Christiano by the smell of his tobacco. "I thought we had an uninvited guest out here."

Christiano took a long drag of his cigarette and nodded. Daniel walked over and placed his hand onto Christiano's shoulder. "You ok, Kid?"

"Arianna's the target."

"Alvarez told you that?"

Christiano got up and began pacing. "Not exactly. We did find Raul though and he finally admitted it was a woman he was contracted to…"

"By whom?"

"I suppose if he wasn't taken out by a sniper, I would have gotten it out of him."

"Shit! A sniper."

"Yeah."

"Do you think maybe it's work related? She does have the kind of job that makes enemies."

"I wish I knew because then it would be easier to find the bastard and kill him." Christiano lit another cigarette.

"I'll double her security. Christiano, I think that maybe you need to tell her now so that she can follow some safety precautions."

"I can't lose her, Daniel."

Daniel patted him on the back. "I know, Kid, I know."

Christiano drove in circles trying to decide if he should tell Arianna about the threat on her life. He finally concluded that Daniel was right, he should tell her so that she could be more careful and protect herself. As he approached her door, he decided that he would savor one last night in her arms before telling her in the morning.

"Chris!" Arianna smiled before throwing her arms around his neck and kissing him.

Christiano walked her backward and kicked the door closed with his foot. Arianna spun them around and pushed Christiano down. "What a welcome!" Christiano smiled.

Arianna pushed off his jacket, opened his tie and started to unbutton his shirt. "I'm going to take care of you. Relax!" Arianna leaned up and kissed him as she unbuckled his belt.

Christiano reached for her hand. "Ari, I…"

"Shhh, I know what you need." She shrugged off his hand, popped open his button and kissed his belly as she unzipped his pants. "Mmm." She grabbed hold of his cock, gave it a few tugs and it sprang to attention. She ran her tongue down his happy trail and then around his throbbing head before going down on him like a starving animal.

Christiano laid his head back, closed his eyes and exhaled. "Oh, Angel!" It wasn't long before Christiano found himself shoving his cock further down Arianna's throat.

Arianna could feel Christiano's legs begin to shake. He was panting and moaning which fueled her to suck harder and faster.

Christiano tried to warn Arianna and pull her away by her hair but she shrugged him off allowing him to cum in her mouth. Once Christiano could speak he pushed Arianna's hair away from her face. "Ari, I…"

"I know you want an encore performance." Arianna smiled.

Christiano leaned down and kissed her. Arianna rose and straddled herself over Christiano. "You're quite talented."

"I have many talents, Mr. Bucati."

"I have some talent of my own." Christiano used his feet to rid himself of his pants.

"I'll be the judge of that." She giggled.

Christiano untied the sash, pushed off her robe and was happily surprised to see that Arianna was completely bare underneath. He ran his hand down her cheek. "You're so pretty."

Arianna wanted to smile but an emotion crossed Christiano's face that made her sad. "Chris, are you alright?"

Christiano nodded before sucking her nipple into his mouth while his hand found its way to her clit. She didn't need to know the truth now.

Arianna's thoughts scattered as Christiano's fingers drove her insane as he slipped them one by one inside her until he pulled her down against his chest and thrust his cock inside her. "AHHH!"

Christiano kissed her and held her tight as he made love to her over and over, until they fell asleep in each other's arms.

CHAPTER 14

Arianna woke to the sound of Christiano's phone ringing. She reached down for his pants to retrieve his phone and instead grabbed his gun. She froze for a moment before dropping it.

Christiano reached for Arianna. "I don't care who's calling."

Arianna got up and pulled on her robe. "I'll be right back."

Christiano sat up. He knew by the look on her face that something was wrong. He reached for his phone to see who could have called to upset her and that is when he spotted his gun. "Damn!"

Arianna threw some cold water on her face and opened the bathroom door.

"Ari, I'm sorry."

Arianna shook her head. "Sorry?"

"I know seeing my gun is what upset you."

"I'm not upset."

"Ari, please don't lie to me."

"Ok, maybe I am a little upset."

Christiano took her hand and kissed it. "I typically take the concealed weapon thing to heart; however, I was thinking with my dick and completely forgot last night when I kicked off my pants."

"It's not like I was shocked. I figured you'd have a gun but seeing it made it a reality."

"It or me?"

Arianna looked down. "You." Arianna wiped a stray tear from her cheek.

Christiano's stomach knotted. He stepped back. "I should go."

Arianna watched Christiano dress, she wanted to say something, but she wasn't sure what to say.

Christiano pulled on his jacket and noticed Arianna standing in the doorway. As he approached her, he paused for a moment. "Take care of yourself, Angel."

The reality of Christiano killing someone with the same gun she saw this morning paled in comparison to the reality of him walking out the door. "Don't go!"

Christiano froze. He closed his eyes willing himself to keep walking, to allow her the life she deserved but instead he turned back toward her. "Ari, as much as I want to…"

"Stay! Please, Chris." Arianna reached for his hand. "I don't want to lose you."

"Ari, I'm never going to change. I will always be the man you suddenly realized I was when you saw my gun. I never want to see you look that way again."

Arianna was in a panic. "I freaked out, I did, but Chris, I'm freaking out more at the thought of you walking out that door and never seeing you again." Tears rolled down Arianna's cheek. "Please don't leave me!"

"Don't cry." Christiano pulled her into a hug and kissed

the top of her head. "If I'm to stay then there's something I need to tell you."

Arianna brewed a pot of coffee while Christiano returned his father's phone call. She watched him through the slider door as he paced and smoked.

Christiano pocketed his phone, put out his cigarette and came inside. "Ari!"

"In the kitchen. Be right in."

Christiano sat and waited for Arianna to come back. He ran through different ways to tell her in his head that someone wanted to kill her. He laughed aloud.

"Did I miss the joke?"

Christiano looked up. "No. I was trying to find a way to… to tell you something."

Arianna handed Christiano a cup of coffee. "Ohhh, do I suck at sex or something?"

Christiano put down his cup, stood and reached for Arianna's hand. "No, not at all. In fact, you're an expert sucker." Christiano winked.

Arianna blushed. "Chris!"

"Come sit."

"Chris, what is it?"

"I have to tell you something."

Arianna sat. "Tell me."

"I should have told you that morning, but I didn't want to worry you. Those men that were outside the house weren't my father's. Someone hired them to watch you, Ari."

Arianna gasped. "Me, why?"

"I wish I knew. I tracked down the man who hired them but before I could find out why, someone killed him."

"My God. So, what you're saying is that someone wants to kill me?"

"Ari, they could just be trying to spook one of us."

"Us? Do you think someone is after me to get to you?"

"Again, I don't know. I have a team of men investigating."

"I think I should call the police."

"Police…"

"You can go, I understand."

"Do you want me to go?"

"No, but…"

"Then I'm staying."

The police were less than friendly to Christiano. He did his best to keep his mouth closed unless asked a direct question but one of the officers was an obnoxious prick and his patience was wearing thin.

The police officer glared at Christiano. "Miss Ricci, have you considered severing your ties with Bucati?"

That was it. Christiano bolted from his seat. Arianna jumped between him and the officer. "Chris, calm down." "No, Officer, it never crossed my mind. Now you can do your job, or you can leave, and I will call your chief."

"We'll look around, question the neighbors and then head back to the station to file a report." The nasty officer walked out.

His partner was a bit kinder. "Miss Ricci, I advise you to keep your doors and windows locked, and don't go anywhere alone. We will be in touch."

"Thank you, Officer." Arianna closed the door and burst into tears.

Christiano finally managed to calm Arianna down enough that she stopped shaking and her tears where slowing down. "I'm going to take care of you, I promise."

"You can't always be with me. We both have to work."

"My men will watch over you while I conduct business."

"Bucati men surrounding the DA's office." Arianna shook her head.

"My men are well trained. They know that they are never to be seen unless it becomes necessary."

"I can't ask you to do that."

"You didn't ask, and they've already been contracted."

"You went behind my back?"

"I did, but in my defense, I thought I'd be able to deal with the matter before you found out. I didn't want you to be unnecessarily worried."

"I can't believe this is happening."

"I have someone who will be here within the hour to install a security and surveillance system."

"WHAT?"

"Look, it's that or come home with me?"

"So, now you're giving me orders?"

"No, I'm keeping you safe, Ari."

Arianna could see how upset Christiano had become. She wrapped her arms around his waist and hugged him. "Thank you."

Christiano walked Arianna into work. He wanted to make sure that Steve knew what was going on. He needed to take precautions not solely for Arianna but for his staff as well, in the event this was work related.

"Can we come in?"

Arianna's boss looked up from his desk. "Of course, Arianna." He extended his hand to Christiano. "Mr. Bucati."

Arianna closed the door. She sat down beside Christiano and held his hand. "I wanted to let you know that…someone is after me. We contacted the police this morning."

"I'm sure the police will be in to ask questions about Arianna's cases in hopes that they can find a lead."

"I will assist them in any way I can. Mr. Bucati, I will arrange to have security keep watch over Arianna and she will be escorted wherever she needs to go."

"I was hoping you'd understand. I've also hired my own men to protect Arianna. All I will need from you is a couple of security uniforms and ID's so that they blend in."

"Yes, Sir, send them to my office when they arrive, and I will personally take care of them."

Christiano squeezed Arianna's hand before letting go to shake Steve's hand. "Thank you. I will let my father know just how cooperative you've been."

"Thank you, Steve."

"Arianna, if you need anything don't hesitate to call me."

Arianna had been on a long conference call which was boring the hell out of Christiano. He decided she would be safe in her office while he went out for a smoke. He waved to her, signaled that he was going for a cigarette and would be back. She nodded. He got in one elevator and Josh got out of the other.

Josh knocked and entered in the same minute. Arianna panicked when she saw the door opening but was relieved to see it was her brother. "What the fuck is going on!"

Arianna covered the phone. "Josh, can't you see that I'm on the phone?"

"HANG UP, ARI!"

"*Excuse me, but I have an emergency and I need to call you back.*" Arianna hung up. "What the hell, Josh?" Arianna got up. She was fuming.

"I heard that the police and your dickhead fuck buddy were at your house today. I called and texted but it seems that you were too busy to reply. Ari, I was scared to death!"

"I'm sorry. I was going to tell you, but I was already late for work and then I had this conference call."

"A simple text would have sufficed."

Arianna reached for her phone. "I'm sorry it's dead. We fell asleep and I didn't charge it last night."

"Why were the police at your house?"

"Someone's watching me or something." Arianna couldn't lie to her brother, so she turned around. She didn't want him to worry any more than he already had.

"Or something? What the hell did that asshole Bucati get you involved in?"

"Josh! Don't talk about Chris like that. It's not his fault. He's gone above and beyond to protect me. He has someone installing a security system in my home and he hired men to guard me."

"You never had any problems until that scum showed up

and now your life is in danger all because you're fucking that criminal."

Christiano was on his way down the hall when he heard yelling coming from Arianna's office, he took off running, pulled his gun, and pushed the door open.

Arianna gasped. "CHRIS, NO!"

"I heard yelling and I…"

"Acted like the criminal you are." Josh smirked at Christiano.

"JOSH!"

Christiano holstered his gun. "I know that you've never liked me, but I care about your sister and I am not going to allow anything to happen to her."

"It looks like it already has and as far as your track record, it looks like you haven't done such a good job protecting the women you claim to care about."

Christiano was seething he reached for his gun but then balled his hand into a fist and gritted his teeth. "If you weren't Ari's brother, you'd already be dead."

"Threatening me, Chrissy?"

"Josh, don't push his buttons." Arianna placed her hands on her brother's chest. "Please, please go. I'll call you later."

"So, this is how it's going to be…you're choosing him over me?"

"No, Josh, we're all upset, and I think we've all said some things that maybe we shouldn't have."

"That's where you're wrong, Ari, I think we said exactly what we meant to say." Josh walked out.

"Thank you for not…"

"Killing your brother?"

"I didn't think you would. I was going to say for not making a bigger scene."

"He's right though, it's my fault Lucia is dead." Christiano wandered back to the corner he had been sitting in earlier and sat in silence.

"I'm sorry that took so long, Chris, I…" Arianna came to a halt when she saw Daniel sitting in her office. "Where's Chris?"

"He needed to take care of a few things, so he asked me to watch over you."

"Dammit! My brother is such a jerk."

"Your brother?"

"He made some awful comment to Chris about him having a poor track record when it came to protecting women he cared about."

"Oh, that would explain his behavior."

"Daniel, how did she die?"

"You should ask Christiano, it's his story to tell."

CHAPTER 15

Arianna called Christiano and left a voicemail when he didn't answer. She spent most of the night up pacing as Daniel slept on her couch. Christiano had obviously given him orders not to leave her side.

"Good morning!"

Arianna looked up from her cup of coffee. "Good morning! Can I pour you some coffee?"

"Yes, thank you."

Arianna grabbed another cup and poured Daniel a piping hot cup of coffee. "Here you go."

Daniel held the coffee up to his nose and inhaled. "Mmm, French press?"

"Yes, unless I'm rushing off to work, then I toss a pod into my Keurig."

"Are you not going to work today?"

"I barely slept. I won't be worth a dime today."

"Arianna, can I give you some unsolicited advice?"

"Of course."

"I've known Christiano for most of his life. He may be his father's son, but he has his mother's heart. He didn't want to have anything to do with his father's business. That's why he moved so far away and tried his best to stay away. Sadly, once Lucia was gone his father preyed on him while he was grieving and angry. The poor kid was in over his head before he realized…look I've said enough. What I am trying to say is, don't give up on him. I see him changing and I know that it's because of his feelings for you."

Arianna couldn't help but smile. "I don't want to give up on him but…"

Daniel stood up and placed his hand onto Arianna's. "Then don't."

Christiano sat in the corner of his room on the floor with Ti amo sprawled out on top of him asleep. He himself had tried to sleep but aside from dozing off a few times, only to wake up from a nightmare, he hadn't gotten much sleep.

There was a knock at Christiano's door, then another. Christiano didn't want to see anyone. He figured if he didn't answer, whoever it was would assume he was asleep and go away.

Arianna opened the door and poked her head inside. "Chris?"

"I want to be alone."

Arianna stepped inside, closed the door behind her and knelt beside Christiano. "Chris, don't push me away."

"Your brother was right…it's my fault she's dead."

Arianna rested her forehead against his. "Oh, Chris…"

"I was driving down the same street we always drove down. We were so in love and talking about our wedding. Suddenly, we were surrounded by SUVs and under fire. I tried to shield her, I did, but…" Christiano wiped his eyes and took a breath. "It was too late. She died in my arms."

Arianna couldn't hold back her own tears. She pulled Christiano into a hug and squeezed him tight. "It's ok. Let it out."

Christiano fell apart in her arms with Ti amo sitting by his side.

"Daniel, where is my son?"

"I think he is feeling a bit under the weather today."

"Have you called the doctor to see him?"

"No, Sir."

"Is Christiano ill, or isn't he?" Giorgio glared at Daniel.

"He's been dealing with some problems and…"

"It's that lawyer he's screwing, isn't it?"

"No. It's Lucia."

"Lucia! She's been dead for years. What now?"

"I think that his feelings for Miss Ricci and the current situation has caused him to relive losing Lucia."

"How could a son of mine be so weak-minded?" Giorgio grumbled in disgust.

"It is not weakness; it is loss of control. You know he has always blamed himself for her death."

"That's nonsense. When he avenged her killers all of his guilt should have been washed away."

There were times when Daniel wished he had killed Giorgio himself to save Christiano from his father's evil ways and right now was one of them.

"You know aside from Daniel; I've only spilled my guts to one other person, and we were shit faced."

"I guess I should feel special." Arianna looked into Christiano's eyes.

"You are so special." Christiano leaned forward and kissed

her. When he pulled away, he stood up and took a step back. "That's why you need to stay away from me."

Arianna sprang to her feet. "WHAT? NO!"

"Ari, don't you understand. I care for you. I won't put your life at risk because I'm selfish."

"You're not being selfish, and you've already done so much to protect me. Chris, I won't walk away from you and I'm certainly not going to run and hide from whomever this is that is after me, or us."

"Nothing I say can force you to leave?"

Arianna laced her fingers through Christiano's. "No, nothing."

"Then you're going to have to adhere to *my* rules."

"Oh?" Arianna stepped back.

"I don't want you going anywhere alone. If I'm not with you then my men will be, and you will follow their orders."

"I promise."

Christiano pulled Arianna into a hug and kissed the top of her head. "How is it that I can be totally unraveled, and you always manage to fix me?"

"I don't fix you, Chris."

"But you do. I can be in the darkest of places and you never judge me. You just drag my pathetic ass back into the light."

"Oh that, well, I do have a thing for your ass." Arianna winked.

Daniel was escorting Arianna to the car when Giorgio pulled up and exited his limo. "Daniel, give us a moment."

"I will go get Christiano's car."

"Hello, Mr. Bucati."

"Arianna, I am concerned about my son. You see, he is allowing your problems to interfere with business."

"I have never asked Christiano to put me before his… work."

"My son, he always feels responsible to take care of those women he allows in his bed."

"With all due respect, Mr. Bucati, your son may be the reason I am in danger. He too, may also be in danger."

"My son can take care of himself."

"Shall I assume that what you would like is for me to take care of myself?"

"My son was correct; you are a smart woman."

Christiano walked out of the house and could see the look of unease on Arianna's face. He yelled out to her. "ARI, DID DANIEL GO FOR THE CAR?"

Arianna turned toward Christiano. "HE DID." When she turned back Giorgio was already walking toward the front door.

Christiano passed his father in the driveway. "Father." His father didn't pause to talk, he nodded and continued walking. Once Christiano reached Arianna, he wrapped his arms around her waist. "What did he say to upset you?"

"Nothing. He's just worried about you."

"He's worried about me?"

"He doesn't want to see you hurt."

"But you'd never hurt me."

"I wouldn't, but whoever is after me could."

Christiano knew that Arianna wasn't telling him the truth, but Daniel pulled up and Arianna took off ending the conversation.

CHAPTER 16

Monica knocked on Christiano's window. He smiled and gave her the one-minute sign with his finger. He quickly finished his call and climbed out of his car. "Hey!"

"I was about to go inside when I saw you. Want to come in and join me for some coffee?"

Christiano glanced at his watch. "Sure, I have a half hour before I have to pick up Arianna."

Monica smiled. "I'm really happy for you."

"It's not like we're getting married or anything. You know we're just…kind of dating."

"Um hmm."

"Sure, we've had dinner…"

"Oh please, you've been having sex with her for weeks, Chris."

"Sex, just sex."

"Are you seriously going to sit there and tell me that you don't have any feelings for Arianna?"

"I…I care about her."

"I knew it."

"There's nothing to know. I care about you too, Monica."

"Yet, you're not having sex with me." Monica smiled.

Christiano rolled his eyes. "That's because you're with Josh."

"So, if I dump Josh, we can have sex?"

"We've already had sex."

"Don't you want more than sex, Chris?"

"Monica, you know my heart will always belong to Lucia."

"I do, but Chris, if she loved you half as much as you still love her then I know that she would want you to find someone to love, someone to love you."

"I've loved two women in my life and they're both dead. I can't lose another."

Arianna finished sorting through her case files, plopped down into her seat and Lynn came walking in carrying a box.

"This was just delivered by messenger. I bet it's a gift from your hot boyfriend." Lynn smiled.

Arianna shook her head. "He is not my boyfriend."

"Whatever, just open it."

"Fine." Arianna pulled the cover off the box and peeled back the tissue paper. Her blood ran cold. "Oh my, God!" She pushed the box away.

Lynn gasped. "I'm calling the police."

Arianna nodded then reached for her phone and dialed Christiano.

Christiano was on his way to meet Rex when his phone rang. He smiled when he saw that it was Arianna calling. *"Hello!"*

"I need you."

Christiano's stomach knotted when he heard the fear in Arianna's voice. *"What happened? Are you alright?"*

"The box."

"Box? Where are you?"

"Work."

"Where are my men?"

"Here."

"Don't move. Stay with my men. I'm on my way." Christiano tripled his speed.

Lynn sat with Arianna in Steve's office while Christiano's men guarded the door.

Steve waited in Arianna's office for the police to arrive. "Officers, thank you for coming so quickly."

"You said that Miss Ricci received a box?"

"Yes, her assistant signed for the box about twenty minutes ago."

"Ok, we will need to speak with her so that we can get a description of the delivery person."

"She's with Arianna in my office."

"I'm going to have my men run through the indoor and outdoor security footage."

Christiano came flying down the hall toward Arianna's office. "Where is she?"

"Mr. Bucati, Arianna is in my office."

"Thank you, Steve."

Arianna ran to the door when she heard Christiano's voice in the hall. "Chris!"

Christiano turned and Arianna leapt into his arms. "He's going to kill me."

Christiano held her in his arms while he kissed the top of Arianna's head trying to calm her. "Shhh, nobody's going to kill you."

"Did they show you what was in the box?"

"No."

Arianna pulled away and looked up at Christiano. "It was a doll; her throat was slit, and she was covered in blood."

Christiano tried to remain calm on the outside for Arianna's sake but he was freaking out on the inside. "Whoever it is just wants to scare you."

"Well, it's working."

"I need to get you out of here."

"I have a hearing this afternoon."

"Miss Ricci, I need to take your statement."

Christiano glared at the officer and then down at Arianna. "You ok to speak to him?"

Arianna nodded. "Will you stay with me?"

"Of course." Christiano took Arianna's hand and led her back to her office.

"No, you don't understand I am *your* boss. What I say goes. I do not take orders from you and if you so much as question my authority again, you will end up with a bullet in your head. Understand?"

Rex stood there with a scowl on his face. "You're a disgrace to the Bucati name."

Christiano lunged at Rex, grabbed his throat, and slammed him into the wall. "Get the fuck out of my sight!"

Rex shrugged away. "Don't you ever lay your hands on me again."

Christiano pulled his gun as Arianna came through the door. "Chris…" Arianna came to a screeching halt when she saw the gun pointed at Rex's head.

Rex stared into Christiano's eyes. "DO IT!"

Christiano holstered his gun, swung around, and reached for Arianna's hand. "Let's go."

Arianna sat quietly in the car while she waited for Christiano to finish talking to Steve. She wasn't sure what had happened between him and Rex, but it sickened her to see him holding a gun to Rex's head.

"I'm sorry that took so long."

Arianna nodded.

Christiano reached his hand over and placed it onto her thigh. "I want you to come home with me tonight."

"I don't think that's a good idea."

"Why not?"

Arianna turned and looked at Christiano. "Your father is why."

"He will understand."

"I'd rather not."

"Ok, then I will stop home and grab a few things and stay with you."

"You don't have to do that."

"Is this about Rex and me?"

"I don't know." Arianna started to cry. "I'm just so scared, Chris."

Christiano hugged her. "I'm going to take care of you. I promise."

Arianna stepped out of the shower to find Christiano pacing. "Is everything ok?"

"Yes, I've been trying to burn off some of this nervous energy."

"I can fix us some dinner or drinks once I finish dressing."

Christiano pulled Arianna into his arms and kissed her. "Why don't you lose this towel and…"

Arianna dropped the towel and kissed Christiano. "Take off your clothes."

Christiano worked on removing his pants while Arianna unbuttoned his shirt. "Much better than pacing."

Arianna walked Christiano backward until his legs were against the bed. "I want to make love to you."

"Ari…"

Arianna shoved him down onto the bed and climbed on top of him. "I need you, Chris."

Christiano pulled her close and kissed her while she made love to him.

CHAPTER 17

Arianna looked out the car window. "Chris, where are we going? We've been driving for almost an hour now."

"I told you it's a surprise. We should be there in about fifteen minutes."

"Thank you for this. I needed a day away from the office."

"I wish it was that easy for me."

"Chris, I know that your father is a powerful man but doesn't being his son count for anything? I mean shouldn't he want to see you happy?"

"My mother did, but my father only cares about himself and the business. I sometimes wonder if he even wanted a child."

"I'm sure he wanted you."

"Yeah, so that I could run the family business after he was gone."

"Will you?"

"I have to."

"Is that what you want?"

"No, but nothing in my life has ever been what I wanted except..." Christiano paused.

"It's ok. I understand. Except for Lucia."

"I'm sorry."

"Chris, she was a part of your life. You can't pretend she wasn't."

"We're here." Christiano was relieved their arrival ended the conversation.

Arianna held her hands over her eyes once they entered the long driveway like Christiano insisted.

Christiano helped her out of the car and walked her a few feet. "Ready?"

"I am."

"Ok, open your eyes."

Arianna opened her eyes and gasped. "Chris, she's beautiful."

Christiano couldn't help but smile wide when he saw happiness and excitement radiate from Arianna. "She's yours."

Arianna looked at the beautiful horse and then at Christiano. "Mine?"

"I bought her for you." Christiano took Arianna's hand. "I named her Cinnamon."

Arianna grabbed Christiano and hugged him. "Oh, Chris, she's beautiful but I…"

"She's yours, Ari." Christiano leaned down and kissed Arianna's forehead.

"I don't know how I can ever thank you."

"That gorgeous smile on your face is thank you enough."

Arianna smiled even wider if that was possible.

Christiano and Arianna rode alongside one another. "I'd forgotten how much I enjoy riding."

"It's been so long for me that I was afraid I'd forgotten how."

"Are you kidding me you're a natural and Cinnamon loves you already."

"I love her too."

"I did my best to find a closer stable, but this was the best I could do."

"What, you mean you haven't arranged for me to bring her home?" Arianna giggled.

"I would have but you told me that you couldn't have any pets." Christiano winked.

"True, I did say that. Seriously, how is this going to work?"

"Cinnamon is yours, and the stable hands will care for her."

"At the risk of sounding ungrateful I don't know if I can afford…"

"Ari, Cinnamon is my gift to you all expenses paid. All you need to worry about is making the time to come and ride her."

"Chris, that's insane. I can't ask you to do that."

"You didn't ask, Ari, I want to do this for you."

"I don't know what to say."

"Thank you works." Christiano smiled.

Arianna fed her horse some apples while she waited for Christiano to finish his phone call. "She really likes you."

Arianna jumped. "Oh, I'm sorry I didn't hear you come in."

"I will try my best to be loud from now on." The man extended his hand. "I'm Bradley."

"Arianna."

"So, are you coming or going?"

"We just came back from a ride." Arianna fed Cinnamon. "Now Cinnamon is enjoying a well-deserved treat."

"How did you know that apples are her favorite?"

"Lucky guess."

Bradley gave Cinnamon a good rub. "She's a beauty." He smiled at Arianna, not the horse.

Arianna couldn't help but stare at Bradley. His shoulders were broad, his jeans way too tight and she had never seen plaid look so enticing. "Yes, beautiful." Arianna smiled.

Christiano stepped into the stable to find Arianna and Bradley smiling at one another. Instantly he became jealous. "Ari!"

Christiano's voice snapped her back to reality. In fact, his tone was one she had rarely heard. "You're back."

"I only left to make a phone call."

Bradley nodded. "Mr. Bucati, I assume?"

Christiano nodded. "And you are?"

Bradley extended his hand. "Bradley Jenkins, we spoke on the phone."

Christiano shook Bradley's hand. "Yes, thank you for taking care of everything."

Bradley glanced at Arianna who smiled. "So, you're the one who helped Chris with his big surprise."

"Guilty." Bradley smiled and stepped back. "Well, I need to get back to work. Nice to meet you both."

"Likewise." Arianna gave him a small wave.

"Bradley, before you go would you mind taking a photo

of my girlfriend and I with her new horse?" Christiano wrapped his arm around Arianna and extended his phone to Bradley.

"Sure thing."

Arianna looked up at Christiano as he pulled her close and stood beside Cinnamon. "Smile, Ari."

Bradley took a few photos before handing the phone back. "Thank you, Bradley."

"No problem, Sir."

Arianna leaned up and kissed Christiano. "I still can't believe you bought me a horse."

"Unfortunately, we need to get going."

Arianna gave Cinnamon a hug and pulled another apple from the sack. "Here you go, Cinnamon. I'll be back soon. I love you, Girl."

Arianna thought that Christiano was acting strange but assumed it was his phone call that left him in a mood. She gave him a few minutes before she tried to lighten his mood. "You know I don't think I've seen you in anything except a suit until today." She admired his dark blue jeans and tight t-shirt that hugged his chest and shoulders.

"I didn't think a suit would be appropriate attire." Christiano stared out at the road.

Arianna expected Christiano to wink or laugh but he didn't. "Chris, are you ok?"

"I'm fine."

"You don't look fine."

"Why because I don't look as good as Bradley?"

Arianna turned in her seat. "That's what this is about? You're jealous of Bradley?"

"I saw how you two were looking at each other."

"Pull the car over."

Christiano kept driving. "Why so you can yell at me and deny it?"

"No, so that I can get out!" Arianna grabbed her purse.

"I'm not going to pull over and allow you get out in the middle of nowhere when your life is in danger."

"If we're in the middle of nowhere then I'm not at risk."

"You are at risk until I find whoever is after you and eliminate them."

"Whatever!" Arianna turned toward the window. She was livid.

Christiano barely had the car in park before Arianna sprung from her seat. She practically ran to her door. Once she was inside, she slammed the door and tossed down her purse.

"Ari, let me in!"

"GO AWAY!"

"Open the door, Ari!"

"Chris, go home!"

Christiano banged against the door. "I'm not leaving. Open the door!"

Arianna rolled her eyes. She knew that he was not going to leave unless the neighbors called the police and had him hauled away for disturbing the peace. She exhaled and pulled the door open.

Christiano entered and closed the door. "Someone may be trying to kill you…"

Arianna huffed as she walked into the kitchen.

Christiano followed. "Now you're not speaking to me?"

Arianna poured herself some water and left the kitchen.

Two hours had passed since Arianna left Christiano standing in her kitchen. She couldn't handle the silence anymore so decided to shower and go to bed.

Christiano heard the shower running. He entered her bedroom, undressed, and slipped into the bathroom.

Arianna was rinsing the shampoo from her hair when Christiano wrapped his arms around her. "I'm sorry." Christiano kissed her neck.

"Chris!" Arianna pulled away.

Christiano grabbed Arianna by her wrists. "I...I can't lose you."

"Then why did you act like a fool?"

"I lost my mind when I saw you looking at Bradley."

"Because you don't trust me?" Arianna stepped out of the shower and wrapped herself in a towel.

"I do. I know that you would never cheat on me but..."

"But what? Say it, Chris!"

"I can never be the man you deserve, I guess I saw him as a threat." Christiano reached for his jeans.

Arianna could see the hurt on Christiano's face, and it broke her heart. As much as she wanted to stay angry, she just couldn't. "Chris, look at me." Christiano looked into Arianna's eyes. "You are the only man I want. When are you going to believe that?" She reached her hand up to his cheek.

"I'm a jerk."

"Yes, you are. Now kiss me you big jerk." Arianna leaned up for her kiss.

CHAPTER 18

"Is everything alright?"

Christiano put down the phone and rolled over. "My father apparently thinks that because I've been staying here for the last few weeks that I need an intervention."

"An intervention?"

"Basically, he'll yell at me and tell me that I don't take the family business seriously and that nothing is more important than family. Then he will belittle me and tell me that I'm weak, and if he's in a bad mood he will go as far to say that I'm a disgrace to the Bucati name."

"You know none of that is the truth, right?"

"Isn't it though?" Christiano sat up.

Arianna sat up and rested her head against Christiano's chest. "If he thinks that little of you, then why do you stay?"

"He's the only family I have left."

"You have me." Arianna gently kissed his chest.

"Sometimes when I'm with you I imagine what it would be like to walk away from him and start over."

"Then do it."

"How? If I so much as try to walk away my father will take me out."

"What if we run away?"

"No, I won't live like that and you have a life here."

"But I love…"

"GET DOWN!" Christiano shoved Arianna down and shielded her with his body.

Glass flew through the room along with a hail of bullets before tires could be heard screeching away. "Chris, what's happening?"

"Stay down, don't move." Christiano pulled the blanket over her, reached for his gun, and ran to the window, but it was too late.

"So, you were in bed and you saw a red beam of light come through the window?"

"Yes."

"Did you see anything else?"

"No."

"What about you, Miss Ricci, did you see anything?"

"No. Christiano threw himself on top of me and told me not to move."

"I'll see if there are any surveillance cameras…"

"Hang on!" Christiano waved his hand at the police officer as he answered his phone. *"Bucati."*

"We lost them, Sir."

"How?"

"They drove across the train tracks and we couldn't make it."

"I trust that you got a plate number and description of the driver?"

"Yes, Sir, we have photos."

"The police are here. I want you to turn around and come back, now!"

"Yes, Sir."

Christiano pocketed his phone as he reached for Arianna's hand. "Officer, my men are on their way back and they have photos."

Arianna stopped two feet from the door. "Are you certain this is the for the best?"

"Ari, I need to keep you safe and right now this is the only place that I can be guaranteed that." Christiano kissed her cheek.

"Ok." Arianna nodded and then followed Christiano into his house.

"Christiano, Arianna, hello!"

"Daniel, would you take Arianna up to her room. I have a few things that I need to discuss with my father."

Daniel nodded and picked up Arianna's bags. "Follow me."

Arianna glanced at Christiano. "I'll be up in a few minutes."

"Hurry."

"You got it."

"Father, may I come in?"

"Enter."

Christiano opened the door, walked in, and sat. "I wanted to thank you for allowing Arianna to stay here with us."

"She is not with *us*; she is with you."

"Why don't you like her?"

Giorgio stood up. "Arianna works for the district attorney's office."

Christiano stood up. "Father, she is not the enemy."

"How do you know?"

"She cares about me."

Giorgio poured himself a drink. "She is making you weak just like…" Giorgio stopped himself.

Christiano stepped in front of his father. "Just like?"

"Christiano, have you forgotten how Lucia made you weak?"

"She didn't make me weak. Lucia encouraged me to follow my dreams."

"DREAMS! Don't you mean run away from your responsibilities?"

"You know how much I've always loved animals and wanted to care for them. So, yes, my dream."

"What about your family, your responsibilities?"

"I'm here aren't I?"

Giorgio shook his head. "Yes, but not by choice."

"Father…"

"I have business to tend to." Giorgio picked up his phone ending his conversation with Christiano.

"If you need anything please feel free to ask."

"Thank you, Daniel."

"Thank you."

"Don't you mean you're welcome?"

"No, I want to thank you for making Christiano so happy. He's had so much pain in his young life, and you bring him joy."

Arianna smiled. "You really care about him?"

"I do. He's the son I never had."

"I know he is very fond of you as well. Daniel, what was Lucia like?"

"I didn't really have the opportunity to get to know her."

"Chris still dreams about her, you know."

"Her death devastated him."

"I know."

"He was lost for a few years but since you've been around, I'm beginning to see the kind, sweet boy he once was."

"I probably shouldn't say this, but he isn't happy working for his father."

"I am aware and so is his father."

"Then why…"

"Family loyalty."

Christiano peeked inside the bedroom. "All settled in?"

Arianna shrugged her shoulders. "I feel like a prisoner."

Christiano pulled her into his arms. "I know but it's the best way to keep you safe."

"What's going to happen when you find him?"

"He will be dealt with."

"So, you will kill him?" Arianna pulled away, walked over to the bed, and sat.

Christiano exhaled. "Ari, why are you worried about someone who wants to kill you?"

"Because killing people is wrong."

Christiano sat and placed his hand on her shoulder. "Look at me."

Arianna looked up at Christiano. "I'm sorry, I…"

"How does the sight of me not repulse you?" Christiano looked away.

"I guess love really is blind." Arianna leaned up, placed her hands onto Christiano's cheeks and kissed him.

Christiano tried to pull away but Arianna straddled herself over him and began kissing her way down his neck. "Ari…"

"Shhh!" She continued down his chest as she scooted herself between his legs and nuzzled her face against his happy trail. "Lay back." She placed her hand on his chest nudging him down. Once he complied, she pulled his stiff cock free and sucked it into her mouth.

Christiano arched his back, grabbed Arianna by her hair and yelled. "Cazzo!"

Arianna knew when he started swearing in Italian that he was close. She sucked his head while she pumped his cock until he came.

Christiano woke with Arianna in his arms looking up at him. "Hey!"

"Did you have a good nap?"

"I can't believe I just passed out like that."

"That orgasm wrecked you." Arianna laughed.

Christiano rolled Arianna over pinning her to the bed. "Now that I'm recharged, it's your turn." He leaned down for a kiss.

Arianna wriggled beneath him. "And he's up!" She smiled.

Christiano pushed up her skirt, yanked her panties to the side and thrust himself inside her. "You're so wet."

"I was thinking about this the whole time you were asleep."

He ripped open her blouse, leaned down and bit her nipple through her bra. "You're so pretty."

Arianna grabbed Christiano's ass and dug in her nails. "I love you, Chris."

"I…" Christiano caught himself before he allowed the words to leave his lips. Instead he thrust harder.

"Oh, God, Chris…" Arianna shook as she exploded with pleasure.

Christiano collapsed beside Arianna is a sweaty heap. "Now we both need a nap." He gasped.

"Chris…"

"I'm sorry, Ari."

Arianna rolled over and rested her chin on Christiano's belly. "Sorry?"

Christiano looked up at the ceiling. "I heard what you said."

"I shouldn't have said it, that wasn't fair. I know you still love her." Arianna rolled away and pulled up the blanket.

Christiano wrapped his arm around Arianna, cuddled up against her, and kissed her shoulder. "Ari, I have feelings for you too."

Arianna wanted so badly to hear him say that he loved her. "Good night."

CHAPTER 19

"IT'S BEEN THREE DAYS!"

"Father, I have done everything that you've asked of me. So, what is this really about?"

"You know I don't trust that woman."

"Well, I do."

"Christiano, you're thinking with your dick!"

"FATHER!" Christiano slammed his hands onto his father's desk.

His father bolted from his seat and grabbed Christiano by his throat. "YOU ARE PATHETIC LIKE YOUR MOTHER!"

Rage raced through him. He pulled his gun and pointed it at his father's head. His voice cracked as his father tightened his grip. "I'd rather be like her, than a monster like you!"

"WHAT IN THE HELL IS GOING ON IN HERE?" Daniel came flying into the room.

Giorgio let go of Christiano's throat. Daniel grabbed Christiano's elbow. "Are you alright." Christiano shook his head before walking out.

"Here you..." Arianna gasped. Christiano was pale, staggering, and holding his gun. "What happened?"

Christiano closed his eyes for a mere second, holstered

his gun and straightened his tie. "I need some air." He continued out to the garden.

Arianna could hear Giorgio and Daniel as their conversation got louder and louder. Her first instinct was to follow Christiano but instead she crept down the hall to hear what they were fighting about.

"For Christ's sake, Giorgio, he's your son."

"Christiano is an embarrassment to the Bucati family name."

"He is still your son. Do you not remember how you felt when he was on his death bed?"

Giorgio chugged down his drink. "Yet, he continues to think with his dick!"

"Why can't you just allow Christiano to have a life of his own?"

"Perhaps if he found the right woman."

"Lucia loved him, and you know how much he loved her."

"Yes, and she tried to keep him in California."

"What about Arianna? She's a beautiful, intelligent woman who cares about Christiano."

"She is either not as intelligent as you think or she wouldn't be wasting her time on my son, unless she has her own agenda and he is playing right into it."

"Giorgio, you broke him once, I don't think he'll survive if anything happens to Arianna."

"You are dismissed." Giorgio turned his back on Daniel.

Arianna ran down the hall before Daniel exited.

Christiano sat smoking in the garden. He couldn't believe that he pulled a gun on his own father. Who had he become?

"Smoking can kill you!"

Christiano glanced up. "I'll take my chances."

"Chris what happened to you? Is Ari ok?"

"She's fine."

Monica reached her hand over and touched the welts on his throat. "Who did this to you?"

Christiano blew out his smoke. "Daddy Dearest."

"Oh, Chris, I'm sorry."

"Me too."

"Do you want to talk about it?"

"Nothing to talk about. We had a fight, he grabbed me by the throat, and I pulled my gun on him."

"And he backed down?"

"Hell no. Daniel came in and put an end to it."

"Thank God because I can't imagine my life without you."

"You and Ari would be better off."

Monica rolled her eyes. "I hate when you say that crap!"

"The truth is the truth."

"Whatever, you'll never change your tune. So, where is Ari?"

"Inside. She's upset with me because I was walking around with my gun. Last time she saw it she freaked out."

"Really? I think it's sexy."

"There's nothing sexy about a gun when it's pointed at your head." Christiano put out his third cigarette and reached for another.

"Before you light up would you mind walking me inside?"

He stuffed the pack of cigarettes back into his pocket and stood up. "I guess I should come along and apologize to her."

123

Arianna paced in her room replaying what she heard, over and over in her head. Could Giorgio be the one who is trying to kill her? Was he responsible for Lucia's death? She needed to get out of there. She grabbed her suitcase and began filling it.

"Knock, knock!" Monica giggled at the door.

Arianna grabbed her and hugged her. "It's so good to see you."

Monica pulled back. "Hey, what's going on? Are you ok?"

"I don't know. Someone is trying to kill me, and I can't help but wonder if it's Chris' father."

"Oh God!"

"I need to get out of here."

"Ari, I think you should talk to Chris first."

"I don't know what happened earlier, but Chris looked awful, he was holding his gun and honestly, he scared me." Arianna broke down.

Monica hugged her while Ti amo laid down at her feet.

Christiano stood in the doorway staring at Arianna's half packed suitcase. "So, that's it, you're leaving me?"

"Come on Ti amo, it's time for a walk." Monica hurried the dog out closing the door behind her.

Arianna turned toward Christiano. "I'm frightened."

"Of me?" Christiano crossed the room closing the distance between them.

Arianna's eyes opened wide. Although, she saw Christiano

earlier, she was so focused on the gun in his hand that she didn't notice the red welts that were now beginning to bruise on his throat. She raised her hand up to his neck. "That's why you had your gun...who did this to you?"

"Don't leave me." Christiano placed his hands onto Arianna's. "I could never hurt you."

"I know that."

"Then why are you packing?"

"Because I can't stay here."

"Did my father say something to you?"

"Chris, I think he's the one who's trying to kill me." Arianna stepped back; she wasn't quite sure how Christiano was going to respond.

Emotions raged through him. Could she be right? Was it his father that was terrorizing her? Until this morning when his father tried to kill him with his bare hands, he may have dismissed the idea but now he wasn't so certain. He dropped down onto the bed. "Yesterday, I would have told you that you were one hundred percent wrong but after what happened earlier..."

"Your father did that to you?"

Christiano felt ashamed and vulnerable, he also felt anger boiling up inside him. "We had a huge argument. He tried to choke me with his bare hands. I thought at first that he was trying to scare me but then I could barely breathe, that's when I pulled my gun. If Daniel hadn't come in, I'd be dead." Christiano let out a sick laugh. "I couldn't pull the trigger."

Arianna kissed Christiano on his cheek and smiled. "I knew you weren't a killer."

"Ari..." Christiano spoke as the door opened.

"Excuse me, Christiano, I need to have a word with you?"

Christiano stood up and exhaled. "I'll be right back. Promise you'll wait for me?"

Arianna nodded. "I promise."

"What is it Daniel?"

"I just received a phone call from Strauss. A familiar face showed up on one of the surveillance tapes we acquired from outside of Arianna's home."

"Who is it?"

"Leo Wright."

"I should have had Carlo kill him when he had the chance."

"It wasn't safe then. You made the right decision to wait."

"Fuck safe, my decision gave him time to come after the woman I..."

"Calm down, Kid."

"I want him found and brought to me."

"Let me take care of him for you, Kid."

"No! He's mine."

"As you wish." Daniel turned and walked away.

Christiano opened the door and Arianna was standing there. "It's Leo?"

"It could be." Christiano held her hand.

"Are you going to kill him?"

"I want to talk to him first."

"First? And then you'll turn him over to the police?"

"We don't need to discuss that now." Christiano turned away from Arianna.

"You're going to kill him, aren't you?"

"If he is responsible, then yes, he will die by my hand."

Arianna's stomach knotted. "Your hand?" Arianna quickly let go of Christiano's hand. She ran back to her room.

"Arianna!"

Arianna shook her head as she threw the rest of her clothes into the suitcase. "I thought I could handle...I need to go, and I don't want you to come with me."

Christiano stepped in front of her. "Do you have feelings for Leo?"

"WHAT! NO!"

"Then why are you so angry with me?"

"Leo deserves to be heard, and if he is guilty, he should go to jail, not be sentenced to death."

"Fine. I will talk to him and if need be, call the police. Are you happy?"

Arianna was relieved to hear that Leo's life would be spared but hearing Christiano's intentions to kill the man made her blood run cold.

"Strauss, unless I give the order he is not to be harmed, understood?"

"Yes, Mr. Bucati."

Christiano opened the door. "Leo!"

Leo was in a chair across from where Christiano sat, his body held in its seat by two men pinning him down by his shoulders. "If you're going to kill me then just fucking do it!"

"Why would you assume I want to kill you? Hmm. Possibly because you've tried to kill Arianna?"

"She deserves what she gets. That bitch got me fired!"

Christiano stood and walked closer to Leo. "No, you got yourself fired because you're a piece of shit who likes to sexually harass women." Christiano lifted his leg, pushed his foot between Leo's legs and applied pressure to his manhood.

"I didn't do anything."

"We have surveillance tape that says otherwise. Strauss, can you show him the footage I viewed earlier."

"Yes, Sir." Strauss hit play.

Leo shook his head. "Fine. I was approached by someone who knew about my situation and offered me a large sum of money to freak her out, but I never intended to kill her."

"Situation?"

"Yeah, I was fired from my job because of her, and I can only assume that I haven't been hired anywhere yet because she has bad mouthed me to anyone who would listen. I fucking hate that bitch!"

"Arianna is too professional to play games and spew dirt about people."

"Guess she has you fooled too." Leo smirked.

Christiano pulled his gun and pressed it against Leo's head. "She asked me not kill you...but I didn't make any promises."

"She did?"

"So, you can decide if you live or die, Leo. You either answer my questions truthfully, or you die. The choice is yours."

CHAPTER 20

"Hey, Sis, ready to hit the slopes?"

"I think I'm going to pass." Arianna looked back down at her book.

Josh dropped down onto the bed beside her. "I don't know exactly what happened between you two and you know I am not a fan of the guy by any means, but, Sis, you're miserable without him."

"I am, but I needed time to think and I feel worse because Chris didn't want me to come."

"Because he'd miss you, or doesn't like us?"

"Christiano feels the need to take care of me. He probably has his men watching the cabin."

"Watching you because he doesn't trust you?"

"No, because he worries about me and my safety. I told you he is a good man."

"Yeah, a good man who is a murderer."

Arianna looked down. "I love him, Josh, I love him so…" Arianna burst into tears.

Josh grabbed Arianna and hugged her. "Ari, if you really love him then make up with the jerk."

"It's not that easy."

"Why not?"

Ari pulled away and wiped her face. "Because as much as I love him, I don't know if I can accept who he is."

"Have you told him that?"

"He knew how upset I was when I left."

"Did he know why?"

Arianna nodded. "I said I needed some time away from him to think."

Christiano was awoken by dog kisses. "Ti amo, hey buddy." He pet his loyal friend. Ti amo rolled onto his back for belly rubs which Christiano happily supplied. "You know I miss her. I never thought that I could ever love…"

"Christiano, is Ti amo in there?"

Ti amo barked.

"Come in."

Daniel poked his head inside Christiano's bedroom. "I've been looking for this guy."

"He apparently followed me in last night."

"I've noticed that you have spent the last few nights out drinking. Do you think that is wise?"

"What else do you suggest?" Christiano sat up.

"Go after her."

"She said…"

"I know what she said. I also know she loves you and how much that scares you. Kid, whether you want to admit it to yourself or not, you love her too."

"Arianna saw a side of me that shocked her into the reality of who I really am."

"Then change who you are."

"How?"

"Start by getting her back."

"Would you like some tea?"

"Tea sounds good. Thank you."

Arianna's mother, Alyssa, placed two teacups onto the table and then poured their tea. "Honey?"

"Do you have any lemon?"

"Fresh squeezed lemon coming right up."

"Thank you, Mom."

"Sweetie, tell me about Christiano."

"I know Josh told you and dad all about the Bucati family."

"News flash! We already knew about the Bucati family. The only thing we didn't know was that you were dating one."

"I guess most people do know of the family."

"What I find surprising is that you'd allow yourself to, as much as, hold a conversation with someone who is on the opposite side of the law."

"I know and I sometimes regret ever allowing myself to stay and talk with him that first time I met him. But then I think about the man I know, and Mom, I love him so much."

Alyssa placed her hand onto Arianna's. "Tell me why you love him."

"He's sweet and kind. Mom, he wants to take care of me. Chris has had a challenging life and maybe that makes me want to take care of him too."

Alyssa smiled as she watched the expressions on her daughter's face as she spoke about the man she loved. "Aside from the obvious, does he have a day job?"

"He is actually a veterinarian and volunteers at local shelters when he isn't busy with his father's hotel business."

"Why doesn't he have his own practice?"

"I once asked him that. He said some people despise him because of his name, and others are afraid, which wouldn't make for good business. But if they ever saw him with an animal, they would never be afraid of him. He loves animals."

"Sweetie, why are you here and what's making you so miserable, if he's so wonderful?"

"I think in the beginning I thought it was kind of exciting that he was a…bad boy, then I saw him in action and reality smacked me in the face. Now, I don't know…"

"He actually kills the people?" Alyssa's eyes opened wide.

"Yes. No. I don't know. I know he has a gun and he told me I deserved better because he wasn't a good person."

"Oh, Ari, the heart always seems to win out, but it seems like your brain needs to get on board."

Christiano buckled into his seat. He decided that he was going to tell Arianna that he loved her and hope that she would give him another chance.

"Five minutes until we take off."

"Thank you, Jay."

Christiano laid his head back and thought about the last conversation he had with Arianna.

"*What did Leo say?*"

"*He confessed.*"

"*He did?*"

"*Yes, and he even sold out the person who hired him.*"

"*Hired him?*"

"*Juan, your old boss.*"

"*Oh God.*"

"*So, what now?*"

"*We took care of it. You're safe now.*"

"What did you do?"

"I had my men find Juan while I waited with Leo for the police."

"Did they find Juan?"

"Yes, and before you ask, when I left him, he was breathing."

"What did you do to him?"

"Ari, don't you know how difficult it was for me to let Leo go, to just walk away?"

"You mean, to do the right thing!"

"That's not fair."

"I need some time and space…away from you."

"Mr. Bucati, can I get you something to drink."

"Black coffee would be great."

"Coming right up."

"Thank you." Christiano looked at his phone, in less than an hour he'd be with Arianna.

Josh and his dad, Jake, were outside shoveling the front steps when Monica pulled up honking. Josh tossed his shovel and darted over to her car. "Hey, Baby!"

Monica hugged Josh. "I've missed you."

"How was the drive?"

"Drive was fine, it went quick. I am starving though."

Jake walked over and hugged Monica. "Welcome to our humble abode."

"Thank you for having me."

Josh grabbed Monica's bag from the car. "Let's eat!"

"My wife made her famous chicken and dumplings."

"Now I'm twice as excited to eat." Monica giggled.

133

Jake opened the door allowing Josh and Monica to enter. "Ari!"

Arianna smiled when she saw Monica. "Hi!"

"I'm going to put down your bag and get cleaned up." Josh kissed Monica. "I'll be right back."

Alyssa wiped her hands and hugged Monica. "Hello, Dear!"

"Oh my gosh, that smells wonderful."

Arianna carried the pot over and placed it down. "Let's eat!"

They were halfway through dinner when there was a knock at the door. "I'll get it." Josh stuffed another bite into his mouth, got up and answered the door. "Oh, Lord."

"I'm here to see your sister."

CHAPTER 21

Josh came back into the kitchen. "Who was at the door, Son?"

"Ari, Christiano is here to see you."

Arianna spit out her food and grabbed her stomach. "Oh, God."

Jake stood up. "Do you want me to ask him to leave, Baby?"

"Josh, show him in. I'll set another place."

"WAIT!"

Monica placed her hand on top of Arianna's. "Do you want me to talk to him for you?"

Christiano stood in the kitchen doorway staring at Arianna and her family. "Excuse me, Mr. and Mrs. Ricci, for intruding but I would like to speak with Arianna."

Jake walked toward Christiano. "I don't think that my daughter wants to speak to you, Mr. Bucati, so I'm going to have to ask you to leave."

Christiano glanced at Arianna who was looking down while Monica rubbed her back. Then back at Jake and nodded. "I'm sorry I interrupted your dinner."

Christiano was hurt that Arianna wouldn't even look at him. He lit up a cigarette as he walked back to his car.

"Are you ever going to quit?"

135

Christiano spun around. "If there's still hope, then I'll never quit."

Arianna took the cigarette from his hand and tossed it into the snow. "I was talking about your smoking habit."

"Ari, forgive me." Christiano reached for her hands.

"There's nothing to forgive. Chris, you've never hidden who you are...I just never wanted to believe it."

"I wish it wasn't who I am, Ari." Christiano looked down at the ground.

"Chris, do you...kill people or do you order your men to?"

Christiano looked away. "Do you honestly want the truth?"

"No, but I need to hear it."

Christiano lit another cigarette. He blew out the smoke. "Both."

Arianna nodded. Deep down she already knew his answer but hearing it aloud sent a shiver through her. How could she love a man who could take someone else's life? "Ok."

Christiano looked at her like she was crazy. "Ok? I confess to murdering people...and you say ok?"

Arianna threw her arms up in the air. "What do you want me to say?"

"That I repulse you to start..."

"But you don't. You should. You're everything I'm against and I shouldn't, but I love you, Christiano Bucati."

Christiano grabbed Arianna and kissed her. He broke the kiss and whispered. "I love you, Ari, I love you."

Arianna stared into his eyes and smiled.

"I don't understand why she ran after him when she didn't want to see him." Jake paced.

Alyssa shook her head. "Honey, she is in love with him."

"I'm worried about her safety. Those people…"

"Dad, I'm not a big fan of Christiano but Ari loves him so I'm trying."

"Why can't she ever love the good guy?"

Alyssa rolled her eyes. "First of all, we can't choose who we fall in love with, and second, Dennis was a good guy. You didn't like him because you caught him climbing in her bedroom window."

"Exactly!"

"You know, Jake, it takes two to tango."

"What's that supposed to mean?"

"Arianna was far from innocent and you made that boy miserable until he escaped and went away to college."

"Quick, come here, look." Monica waved for them to come over to the window.

Christiano kissed Arianna. "Now what?"

Arianna smiled. "I don't know but I don't want to lose you."

Christiano's eyes filled with tears. "Good because I can't lose you, Ari."

"Are you crying." Arianna reached her hand up and wiped away a stray tear that rolled down his cheek.

"I didn't think I could ever love someone the way that I love you."

"I don't understand. I know how much you loved Lucia."

"I do…I did, but, Ari, she only knew one side of me. I was not the man I am now. Things were simple with Lucia, so much so, that sometimes I wonder how long we would have lasted in the fairytale I created for us."

"To avoid your father?"

"Him, and this life."

"I know why you came back but, Chris, why did you stay?"

"I ask myself that every damn day. I was so broken I couldn't function and then…" Christiano paused as the memory of his first kill ran through his head. "It was too late."

"Chris, it's never too late."

Christiano reached his hand up and ran it down Arianna's cheek. "You almost make me believe that."

"Believe it." Arianna leaned up and kissed him.

"I think I will go set another place at the table." Alyssa headed toward the kitchen.

"Well, I'm going to have them come inside. I cannot imagine what the neighbors are thinking. First, he arrives in a limo with his entourage, and now he's on the front lawn allover your sister."

"Dad, wait. You'll just upset Ari if you go out there."

"She should have known better than to get involved with someone like him."

"I know but, Dad, she's in love with him."

"He's in love with her too."

"Monica!"

Monica looked at Josh and shrugged. "What? It's true."

Jake gritted his teeth and opened the door.

Arianna and Christiano were kissing when Christiano felt a firm hand on his shoulder. His instincts kicked in, he swung around shielding Arianna with his body and reached for his gun before realizing it was Jake.

Jake gave him an awful glare. "Catch you off guard, Mr. Bucati?"

Arianna stepped out from behind Christiano. "Daddy!"

"I'm sorry, Sir, and please call me Christiano." Christiano extended his hand.

Jake looked down at his hand and out of the corner of his eye he could see Arianna giving him the same glare he had just given Christiano. He extended his hand to Christiano. "Jake."

Arianna laced her fingers through Christiano's. "Why don't we go back inside." Arianna pulled Christiano toward the house.

Her father stood there a moment composing himself for the long night ahead of him.

"Mom, they are on their way back in and dad does not look happy."

"He never has when your sister brought a boy home."

"Christiano is more than your typical man."

"So are you, Josh." Monica smiled and planted a big kiss on Josh's lips.

"Yeah, what's that supposed to mean?"

"You're special."

"I know he's your friend but please, don't ever compare us. The thought that my sister allows him to touch her makes my skin crawl. Thank God you never…"

Arianna burst through the door with Christiano in tow. "Mom, would you set another place at the table please."

"Already done, Dear." Alyssa walked toward Christiano and smiled. "Come, sit and have dinner with us."

"Thank you, Mrs. Ricci."

Alyssa nodded. "Please, call me Alyssa."

"Thank you, Mom."

Josh waited as Monica followed them to the kitchen. "I thought you two were going to brawl out there."

"I was not expecting him to react that way or let it be known that he was carrying a gun."

"Always."

Jake closed his eyes and exhaled. "What are we going to do?"

"How can we do anything when Ari is in love with him?"

"She'll never be DA with him by her side."

"Come on, you two." Alyssa stood there waiting for them to move toward the kitchen.

Christiano ate every bite. "That was absolutely delicious. I haven't had a meal like that since my mother became too ill to cook."

"Oh, I'm sorry."

"Thank you."

"So, what do you do?"

Arianna practically choked on her wine. "Excuse me."

Jake motioned his hand. "Look, we all know what the Bucati name stands for, so let's get that out of the way right now…"

"DAD!"

Christiano reached for Arianna's hand. "It's ok. I understand how you feel, Sir, and I appreciate that you love Arianna so much that you've allowed me into your home. Aside from what you may have read or heard; I do work for my father's hotel business."

"Would that be a legitimate business?"

Arianna sprung up, tossed down her napkin and looked at her father. "That's enough!"

"I'm concerned about you, Arianna."

Arianna shook her head. She was disappointed and ashamed of her father's behavior. "Take me home, Chris."

Christiano stood up and paused for a moment before following Arianna. "I want you to know that I would never hurt your daughter, I'd give up my life for her because I love her."

Christiano walked out leaving Arianna's family staring at one another in silence.

"Hey, Angel!" Christiano held Arianna in his arms and kissed her forehead.

"Chris, I'm so sorry they treated you that way."

"It's ok."

"No, it's not. You're a good man."

"Am I, Ari?"

"You're good to me."

"I wouldn't want my daughter to date me."

"They didn't even get to know you."

"All that matters, is that you know me."

"And I love you." Arianna kissed Christiano. "It will only take me a few minutes to pack up and then we can leave."

"You can't leave."

"I don't expect you to stay with the way they treated you and I am certainly not going to stay without you."

Christiano placed his hands onto Arianna's shoulders. "I won't come between you and your family. I know how much they mean to you."

"Well, if they felt the same way they would have welcomed you."

"They tried but their feelings are valid and…"

Arianna shrugged away. "I can't believe you! You're going to defend *them* now?"

"I came here to apologize and tell you that I love you. Not, to cause trouble which, I inadvertently did." Christiano lifted Arianna's chin up so that he could look into her eyes. "Ari, I won't ask you to choose between me and your family. You need to talk to them and find a common ground."

"What about you?"

"I'll be ok as long as you work through this with your parents."

"Why is my family so important to you?"

"Because I know what it is like not to have any. My father is a curse and I would do anything to have even five minutes with my mother. Don't waste what you have. They love you, Angel."

Arianna hugged Christiano. "I don't deserve you."

"No, you don't, you deserve better but I'm a selfish prick remember." Christiano laughed.

"Will you come downstairs with me?"

"I think you should talk to them alone."

"You're probably right."

"I'll walk you back down but then you talk to them and I will wait outside. I need a smoke and have a few calls to return."

Arianna opened her door and gasped.

Alyssa and Jake jumped back when Arianna pulled the door open, but it was too late they were caught eavesdropping. "Oh...uhh, your father and I were just..."

"Mom, you and Dad were eavesdropping!"

Jake stepped forward. "I was afraid that Christiano would take his anger out on you."

"Dad! He's not like that."

"So, we heard." Jake extended his hand. "I'm sorry. We judged you before we allowed ourselves to get to know you. While I am quite embarrassed, I am also relieved that you understand how we feel, and that you know the importance of family."

Christiano nodded. "I do, Sir."

"I'm sorry too. How about we all go downstairs, have some pie, and start over?"

Christiano looked down at Arianna.

Arianna wrapped her arm around Christiano's waist. "Ok."

He leaned down and kissed her on the top of her head. "I told you they love you."

CHAPTER 22

Three weeks later…

"What would you like for dinner tonight?"

Arianna turned in Christiano's arms. "You!" She winked.

"You'll need your energy then, so what is it, Italian, French…?"

"Anything as long as I get dessert when I clean my plate." She giggled.

"You're no help."

"Since it's so important that I choose, I pick Italian." Arianna placed her hand on Christiano's bulge. "I have this thing for cannoli."

"Oh, do you?" Christiano smiled."

"Yes, and I can't wait for dessert."

Christiano hopped out of the bed. "Ok, be ready in an hour."

"An hour?"

"Yes."

"Is it breakfast or dinner?"

"You ask too many questions."

Arianna opened her mouth but Christiano stuck his tongue in making her forget everything for a moment except for his warm, hard body pressed against hers.

"Chris, why are we entering the airport?"

"You requested Italian food, didn't you?" Christiano smiled a huge smile.

"I did but…" Arianna gave Christiano a questioning look."

"No buts! We have reservations at my favorite restaurant. The pasta is homemade, the gelato is incredible, and the cannoli is to die for."

"Your favorite restaurant is here at the airport?"

Christiano laughed. "No silly, but my plane is here, and Jay is awaiting our arrival to fly us there."

Arianna's mouth dropped open. "Fly us?"

"Yup!" Christiano maneuvered through the parking lot and pulled up to the hangar where his plane is housed.

"Chris, are you crazy?"

"For you." Christiano leaned over and kissed Arianna. "And pasta."

"Are we actually flying to Italy?"

"Yes, Matera to be exact."

"My God, so if I said French food we'd be on our way to Paris?"

"Would you prefer we go to Paris?"

"No, I'm all about pasta…and your cannoli." Arianna winked.

Arianna was captivated by the view outside her window. "The sunset is gorgeous."

Christiano kissed her cheek. "It pales in comparison to my view."

Arianna smiled and kissed Christiano. "I love you."

145

"I love you too." Christiano dropped down into his seat.

"I've never been to Italy."

"My mother would bring me twice a year to visit her family. Sometimes we would stay for a month and sometimes the whole summer."

Arianna could see the sadness in Christiano's eyes. "I'm sorry I didn't mean to upset you."

"No, you didn't upset me. Those were some of the best memories I have of my mother."

"Is this the first time you've been back?"

"I've been to Rome, Venice, Milan, and Matera several times but once my mother died the visits to Sicily ended."

"Why?"

"My mother's family never accepted my father. For a while they even disowned my mother but once I was born, they reconnected."

"So, you haven't seen them in twenty some odd years?"

"I called my aunties a few times before my father caught on and put an end to it."

"But, Chris, you could have contacted them when you got older."

"I thought about it but to be honest, I was afraid."

"Afraid of your father finding out?"

"Well, that, but also the thought of them rejecting me."

"But why would they? You're their blood too."

"Yes, but my father's runs through my veins as well."

"Then I am certain they will understand your reluctance to contact them sooner."

"I'll think about it."

The limo pulled up in front of a beautifully landscaped villa. "This hotel is beautiful."

"It's not a hotel. I hope you don't mind but I thought the villa would give us more privacy and be more secure."

"The whole place is ours?"

Christiano stepped out of the limo and extended his hand to Arianna. "Yes."

"I bet it will look even more exquisite in the bright daylight tomorrow."

"I'm sure. The backyard has a man-made pond and a flower garden."

Arianna hugged Christiano. "How about we check out the bedroom?"

Christiano leaned down for a kiss. "Ahh, I'll show you, but we need to change quickly in order to make our dinner reservation."

"Can't we have dessert first?" Arianna pouted.

"As tempting as it sounds, which it does, dessert will have to wait until after dinner."

"I don't think I've ever consumed so much food." Arianna held her stomach.

"I warned you that once you tasted the pasta it was all over."

"The olives, calamari, cheeses, eggplant, and the salad were just delicious."

"Don't look now but your cappuccino and dessert platter are on the way."

Arianna's eyes opened wide when she surveyed the dessert

platter. It held gelato, cannoli, amaretto cheesecake, custard filled zeppole, and warm biscotti. "I've gained ten pounds and haven't even tasted a thing yet!"

Christiano chuckled. "You must taste them all even it is only a small bite of each."

Arianna handed Christiano a spoon. "Let's start with the gelato."

Christiano dug his spoon into the pistachio gelato. "Open up!"

"Oh God, this is so good."

"Here try the zeppole."

"I'm ready for some cannoli."

"I thought we'd wait until we were back at the villa." Christiano laughed and pushed the zeppole into her mouth.

"I'm in love!" Arianna giggled.

Christiano leaned over the table and ran his tongue across her lips to lick up the cream that escaped her zeppole. "So am I."

As they made their way up the driveway Arianna could see a golden sort of glow coming from what she assumed was the garden. "Chris, why is the garden so brightly lit?"

"I don't know."

Arianna held Christiano's hand as he walked them to the door. "Maybe we should check?"

Christiano nodded as he pushed the door open. "Sure."

Arianna stepped inside, looked down and then back at Christiano. "What is this?"

Christiano shrugged. "I don't know."

Arianna looked at the trail of rose petals on the floor. "Chris, tell me?" She smiled.

"Nope, you'll have to follow the path and find out for yourself."

Arianna started off slowly but as her curiosity got the best of her she quickened her steps until she reached the garden. The garden was full of roses and tiny white lights hanging from the rose covered trellises. Arianna spun around. "Chris, it's…"

Christiano dropped to his knee and took hold of her hand. "Ari, until I met you my life was black and white and now it's filled with color and happiness. I love you, Arianna, with all my heart and soul…marry me?"

Arianna stood there frozen, her hands shaking as tears filled her eyes. She nodded. "I love you so much."

Christiano stood up. "Is that a yes?"

Arianna wrapped her arms around Christiano's neck. "Yes, a hundred times, yes! I love you."

Christiano twirled her around before placing her back down onto her feet. He pulled a ring from his pocket and slipped it onto her finger.

Arianna looked down at the large emerald cut diamond ring. "It's so beautiful."

"You'll always outshine any diamond in my eyes." Christiano lifted her hand to his lips and kissed it.

CHAPTER 23

"Chris, why are you so nervous?"

"Talking to my father is like playing Russian roulette, you never know what you're up against."

"I understand. I was afraid that my father was going to go crazy, but he actually sounded happy for us."

Christiano pulled Arianna against him and kissed her forehead. "Your father already knew."

"You told my father?"

"I asked him for his permission."

"You did?"

"Of course, I did."

"Oh, Chris, that was so sweet."

"It's not sweet, it's the right thing to do."

"I am a bit shocked that he said yes."

"Thanks for the vote of confidence." Christiano laughed.

"He did tell me all my life that I wasn't allowed to date until I was thirty."

"He did seem reluctant but, in the end, he gave me his blessing along with a threat to kill me with his bare hands after removing my manhood with a rusty knife, if I ever hurt you."

Arianna giggled. "Well, that does seem fair."

"I'd never hurt you, you know that, right?"

"I do."

Christiano took Arianna's hand. "Let's do this."

Ti amo practically tackled Christiano to the floor when he heard him come in the door. Christiano dropped down and gave his furry four-legged friend a hug. "Hey, Buddy."

Arianna knelt and gave Ti amo some love as well. "Aww, he missed you."

"Christiano, you've returned."

"We have. Is father home?"

Daniel nodded. "He's in his office."

"I need to have a word with him. Do you think now's a good time, or should I wait?"

"If it's about that ring on Arianna's finger then perhaps sooner is better than later. You know all too well how he will react if he hears it from someone else."

Christiano was beaming. "It is. You were right, Daniel, you told me one day I'd find someone who made me feel whole again."

Daniel was beaming. "I'm so happy for you, Kid." He extended his hand but Christiano grabbed him and gave him a hug. "Congratulations to you too, Arianna."

Arianna looked up at Daniel. "Thank you, Daniel. I'm not sure if we would have made it without you."

Daniel smiled at Arianna. "True love always finds a way."

Arianna held Christiano's hand. "I guess it does."

"I will let your father know you'd like to speak with him." Daniel knew how Giorgio was going to react and it made his stomach knot.

"Hello, Father."

Giorgio sat at his desk staring at Christiano. "Sit."

"Yes, Sir." Christiano sat.

"I heard that you were in Italy the last few days."

"I was."

"Perhaps you've forgotten that you work for ME?"

"No, Father."

"There was business to take care of and where were you… halfway around the world with that…"

Christiano stood up. "Don't you dare!"

Giorgio stood up, placed his palms down on his desk and glared at Christiano. "Speak the truth? That she is nothing but a money hungry whore, who has her own agenda!"

Christiano balled his hands into fists. If it weren't that he wanted so badly to see the look on his father's face when he told him his news, he would have slugged him right then and there. He allowed a slight grin to cross his face. "I'll have you know that I asked her to marry me while we were in Italy."

Giorgio's face turned red with anger. "CALL IT OFF! YOU WILL NOT MARRY HER!"

Arianna was waiting for Christiano in the living room with Ti amo. "I'm going to be your mommy now, Ti amo." She rubbed his belly. "You like that don't you?"

"I'm certain he does."

"I hope so. I know how much Chris loves this big guy." Ti amo licked her hand.

"I'd venture to say that he loves you a tad more." Daniel smiled.

"I love him too."

"I know you do."

Arianna opened her mouth to speak when Ti amo jumped up barking. He took off toward Giorgio's office. Arianna and Daniel followed.

"YOU CANNOT TELL ME WHAT TO DO!"

"THE HELL I CAN'T!"

"I LOVE HER!"

"YOU'RE A FOOL!"

"YOU THINK THAT CALLING ME NAMES IS GOING TO MAKE ME CHANGE MY MIND?"

"YOU HAD BETTER END IT OR YOU WILL REGRET IT!"

Daniel opened the door and Arianna rushed to Christiano's side. "Come on let's go."

Christiano nodded and laced his fingers through Arianna's left hand allowing the sparkle of her ring to glare at his father.

Giorgio took notice. "Ms. Ricci, you may have my son fooled but you will never fool me. Now get the hell out of my house! You are not welcome here!" Giorgio turned his back.

Christiano was far from finished saying what he wanted to his father, but he didn't want to upset Arianna any more than she already was, so he gritted his teeth and walked away.

Christiano headed straight for his room. He pulled his suitcases from the closet and tossed them onto his bed. "I'll get the closet; do you mind emptying the drawers?"

Arianna stepped in front of him. "Hey, maybe you should calm down before you do something you can't undo."

"Aren't you the one who keeps asking me to walk away?"

"Yes, but not like this. No good decision has ever been made in anger."

"You're right." Christiano dropped down onto his bed.

Arianna rubbed his back. "Come home with me tonight and give your father some time to cool down."

"Ok, but we have to take Ti amo with us. I'm not comfortable leaving him here with my father so angry."

"You think he'd hurt him?"

"Possibly, and I'm not willing to chance it."

"But I'm not allowed pets."

"We'll sneak him in and if we get caught, I'll buy us a new house tomorrow."

Arianna shrugged her shoulders. "I've been wanting to move anyway."

"Good, because I plan on buying us a beautiful house with lots of bedrooms and a huge yard for our children to play in."

"Lots of bedrooms, huh?"

"You don't want children?"

"I do, but how many is lots?"

"Three or four."

Arianna smiled and kissed Christiano. "Maybe we should start practicing tonight?"

Christiano grabbed her ass, pulled her close and kissed her.

Giorgio poured himself a drink, sat down at his desk and looked up. "Daniel, why are you still here?"

"Christiano is your son. Do you really want to chase him away?"

"That woman makes him incompetent. All she is after is his money."

"I believe she honestly loves him."

"It doesn't matter what you or my son believe, Arianna Ricci is about to have a terrible accident."

"You can't kill her!"

"EXCUSE ME!"

"What I mean is all fingers will point to you. You need to wait it out some, for your sake."

Giorgio took a gulp of his drink. "Perhaps you're right."

"Maybe even pretend to make amends, so that you can do as you did when you had Lucia taken care of and grieve beside your son. It made your bond stronger."

"Yes, and this time the hit needs to be when Christiano is out of harm's way. Those fools almost killed him too."

"Brilliant idea."

"Perhaps a shooter at the courthouse."

Daniel was horrified but relieved that he bought Arianna some more time. Now how was he going to save her?

Christiano sat staring at the wall. Arianna knew he was upset and felt guilty that she was the cause. She poured them each a drink and sat beside him. "Here you go."

"I'm sorry that my father ruined everything."

"I hate that I've come between you and your father."

Christiano placed his hand onto Arianna's cheek. "My mother would have loved you."

"I'm sure I would have loved her as well."

"Everybody loved her."

Arianna rubbed Christiano's thigh. "Why don't we head to bed. It's been a long day."

Christiano finished his drink, kissed Arianna's forehead, and then took her hand. "Long day or not, you never have to talk me into taking you to bed."

Arianna was sound asleep in Christiano's arms. He tried to sleep but couldn't. His anger towards his father was beginning to diminish only to be replaced by hurt. Why couldn't his father trust his judgement or be happy for him? Did he even love him?

"Can't sleep?"

"You were snoring too loud."

Arianna bit his nipple. "Jerk!"

"Hey now!" Christiano rolled Arianna onto her back.

She placed her hands on his cheeks. "You know you're going to get through this and I'm going to be with you every step of the way."

"I love you, Ari." Christiano trailed kisses up and down Arianna's body before he slid himself inside her. It was only then that he was at peace.

CHAPTER 24

Christiano paced back and forth as he hovered his finger over the send button on his phone. He couldn't believe that his contacts had found his aunts so quickly. His first instinct was to run to the phone, then his nerves kicked in...what if they didn't want to hear from him or worse, what if his father found out? To hell with his father. The best memories he had of his mother were of the times they spent in Italy with his aunts. He hit send and waited as the phone rang.

"*Ciao!*"

"*Ciao! Hello, I am the son of Bella...*"

"*CHRISTIANO?*"

"*Yes. It's me, Zia Tina!*"

"*Oh, Christiano, my little orsacchiotto. I've prayed every day that you would call us.*"

"*Father wouldn't allow me for many years. I know I should have tried to find you sooner but...*"

"*You've found me now. I cannot wait to tell Angela and Gia you are well. You are well, no?*"

"*I'm well.*"

"*You will come visit soon?*"

"*I will come soon and if it is alright, I have someone special that I would like for you to meet.*"

"*Oh, Christiano, you're in love how splendid.*"

"*Arianna reminds me of my Ma-Ma. Zia, she loves me so much.*"

"*As she should. Orsacchiotto, we will count the days until we hold you in our arms.*"

"*I promise it will be soon.*"

"*Until then. Arrivederci, my precious orsacchiotto.*"

"*Arrivederci, Zia Tina.*"

Arianna rolled over to find the bed empty. She pulled on her robe and set out to look for Christiano. As she entered the living room, she could hear him talking on the phone. She stopped and listened for a moment. When she realized he must have been speaking with one of his aunts she couldn't help but smile. Arianna stepped inside the kitchen as Christiano told his aunt that she reminded him of his mother. Her heart swelled with joy.

Christiano ended his call, put down his phone and wiped his eyes. Before he was able to turn around Arianna wrapped her arms around his waist. "I found you."

"I, uh, I called my aunt." He sniffled.

Arianna turned him in her arms. "Hey, are you crying?"

"Happy tears I suppose. You know I never noticed how much her voice sounded like my mother's."

Arianna reached up and wiped away his tears. "I know how much you miss her."

"It feels like an eternity since she left me."

"You know when my grandmother died my mom told me that loved ones never leave us, they just live in here and here." She tapped his head and kissed his chest over his heart.

Christiano hugged her and kissed the top of her head. "I love you."

"You really didn't have to walk me into work."

Christiano opened Arianna's door and held it for her to walk in. "I know but I wanted to."

"Are you stalling so that you don't have to see your father?"

"That too."

"I'm sorry."

"It's not your fault. I just don't know what to do."

"I'll support you whatever you decide."

"I wish I knew how to walk away."

Arianna closed her door. "Chris, what if I put you in contact with some people and…"

"I can't turn on my father as much as I want to be free."

"What if we move. Go back to Italy and live there?"

"You mean run and hide? My father will find us. Ari, I don't want to spend the rest of my life looking over my shoulder."

"Then you had better go make peace with him."

"I suppose I don't have a choice."

Arianna hugged him extra tight. The thought of him more than likely having another fight with his father gave her an awful feeling. "Will you call me after you talk to him?"

"I will call you every five minutes if you'll feel better about me leaving."

"I'm fine."

"Yet, you're squeezing me like you're never going to see me again."

"Guess I'm a little worried."

"Well, I plan to have Daniel on standby."

"Ok."

Christiano kissed Arianna and then he was gone.

Daniel sat waiting for Christiano in the garden. He wasn't certain that anything he said could stop Giorgio from killing Arianna, but he would be damned if he was going to sit by and watch. Giorgio destroyed Christiano's life once and he wouldn't be silent again. Christiano deserved to be happy.

Christiano stepped between the bushes into the garden. "Hey, thank you for meeting me out here." He lit a cigarette and offered one to Daniel.

Daniel took a cigarette. "So, Kid, I'm not sure your father is going to back down on this."

"I thought all night long about this and if we can't come to a common ground, I'm going to give him an ultimatum."

Daniel cringed. Giorgio didn't like to be threatened but an ultimatum was asking to be crucified. "Kid, your father wants what he wants."

"Well, then I hope it's to keep me in his life because otherwise I will pack up and leave."

"It won't be that easy."

Christiano could see how rattled Daniel looked. "You really don't think there is a way around this, do you?"

"No, I don't."

"Then wish me luck." Christiano flicked his cigarette to the ground and stomped on it.

Giorgio knew that Christiano was standing in his doorway, but he didn't bother to look up.

Christiano cleared his throat. "Father, may I have a word?"

"Have you come to apologize?"

"Father, why can't we ever have a civilized conversation like a normal father and son?"

Giorgio snapped his head up and glared at Christiano. "Normal sons wouldn't disrespect their father by yelling at them or pointing a gun at their head!"

"With all due respect, you were choking me."

"And if Daniel hadn't removed you, I may have killed you."

Christiano nodded. "Nice."

"Christiano, why do you feel the need to challenge me and my judgement? Do you think that my empire was built on disrespect and lack of loyalty?"

"Father, just because I do not agree with you does not mean that I don't respect you."

"If it were a business matter, I would discuss it, but it is about that woman..."

"She isn't some woman, Father, I love her. I haven't been this happy since my mother was alive."

Daniel had stepped inside the room shortly after Christiano. He looked at Giorgio willing him to play into Christiano's plea for happiness. He knew that if Giorgio followed along, he would only be putting on an act so Christiano would not be suspicious when Giorgio had Arianna killed. However, Daniel had his own plan.

"Daniel, pour my son and I a drink."

"Yes, Sir."

"Come sit." Giorgio walked Christiano over to the couch and sat. "You loved Lucia as well, did she not make you happy?"

"She did."

"Then how can you be certain that you love this woman?"

"It's different. With Lucia I was happy, and I loved her but… Arianna makes me feel alive again. I am no doubt in love with her, heart and soul."

Daniel handed them each a drink.

"There will be a prenuptial agreement and I want an NDA."

Christiano blinked and saw Daniel nod out of the corner of his eye. "Yes, Sir."

"If she tries to come between us or cause trouble, I will take matters into my own hands."

"Understood."

Giorgio raised his glass. "Then we have come to an agreement."

Christiano glanced up at Daniel in disbelief and then back at his father. "Thank you, Father."

Arianna couldn't eat or drink she was sick to her stomach with worry.

"Hey, Sis!"

"Hey!"

"What's up with you?"

"Busy. How are you?" Arianna looked away hoping her brother would believe her lame excuse.

"Me…well, right now I am upset about my sister."

Arianna rolled her eyes and looked back toward Josh. "I'm worried about Christiano."

"Why is he out killing someone?" Josh laughed.

"JOSH!" Arianna gritted her teeth.

"Sorry, I was only joking…not. Look, a guy in his line of work is walking a fine line every day."

"I know but today he is discussing us with his father."

"Oh, so big man Bucati doesn't approve of you two?"

"No, he doesn't."

"Well, I don't approve of his son, but I love you so…"

"Yeah, but you're normal."

"You think I'm normal?" Josh rolled his eyes and made a funny face.

Arianna giggled. "Ok, more normal than he is."

"Least you laughed."

"Want to go grab a cup of coffee?"

"Sure, I have some time before my next meeting."

Christiano walked outside with Daniel following. "So, what trick do you think he has up his sleeve?"

"I didn't think you bought that, but you played along quite well."

"If he's trying to dig up dirt on Arianna or her family, he isn't going to find any."

"At this point, if he tried to blackmail you it wouldn't surprise me."

"I wish I could disappear with Arianna."

"What if you could?"

"He'd find me, and I couldn't ask Arianna to leave her family for me."

"Then strike a deal with…"

"No! As much as I hate him at times, he is still my father."

"Then please, be careful, Kid."

"I will…and, Daniel, thank you. You've been more of a father to me than he ever has."

"I promised your mother that I'd take care of you. A promise is a promise." Daniel nodded.

"I miss her."

"Me too, Kid."

Christiano sat waiting in his car for Arianna to finish work. After he met with his father, he texted to say that all was well, and he had survived. Shortly thereafter, he went searching for houses. He found the perfect home and was excited to take Arianna to see it.

"Hey, Cutie!"

Christiano smiled. "Hop in!"

"Yes, Sir!" Arianna giggled.

"I went house hunting today and I think I found…"

"You went looking for houses without me?"

"Ut-oh. I thought you'd be as excited as I am."

"It's not that I'm not excited to have a house with you, it's just that we didn't get to do it together."

"Ok, how about this…if you don't like the house we can keep looking or we can start over?"

"Why don't we go see this house you're in love with and then come up with a plan."

"I'm in love with you, not the house. I will live anywhere that you choose. I love you."

"I love you too, now drive. I want to see what you found."

Arianna was expecting Christiano to pull up to a huge mansion but instead he pulled up to a ranch style house. It was by no means small but far from a mansion.

Christiano watched Arianna's expression as they pulled into the driveway. "So?"

"The exterior is beautiful."

"Would you like to see the inside?"

"You have the key?"

"The realtor gave it to me."

"Yes!" Arianna popped open her seatbelt and practically ran to the front door.

Christiano followed her up onto the porch. "Turn and look at the view."

Arianna spun around and gasped. "I didn't realize you could see the lake from here."

"Picture us sitting on the porch in these rockers watching the moonlight sparkle off the lake." Christiano wrapped his arms around Arianna's waist.

"SOLD!"

"Ha-ha, you need to see the inside before you decide if this is the one."

"Ok!" Christiano opened the door. "Wood floors and a fireplace."

"Three fireplaces. There's one in the family room and another in the master bedroom."

"I've always wanted a kitchen with a breakfast nook."

Christiano walked her to the slider door and out onto the back deck. "We'd need to install a fence for Ti amo."

"What a gorgeous garden, oh, and a pool!"

"The far end of the pool has a hot tub."

"I want to see more."

Arianna went back inside and explored all three bedrooms before entering the last one which was the master bedroom. She opened the door to find candles, flowers, and a bucket of champagne. "Chris…" She wandered inside.

Christiano hugged her. "I love you."

"I love you too, and our house."

"Our house?"

Arianna nodded. "Yes, now let's christen it." She smiled.

"I'm up for that." He leaned down and kissed her before scooping her up and carrying her over to the bed.

CHAPTER 25

"Why are you so nervous?" Arianna looked up from the floral arrangement. "Because your father is coming to our home for dinner and he will be meeting my family!"

Christiano pulled her hands from the flowers and held them. "Angel, your family loves you and so do I. I'm the one who should be nervous."

"You?"

"After meeting my father, your father will probably revoke his blessing to marry you."

Arianna kissed Christiano. "It's way too late for that."

Christiano smiled. "Yes, it is." He kissed her. "You know if you stop fussing over those flowers, we may have just enough time for a quickie."

Arianna glanced at the flowers. "They look good to me." She smiled.

Christiano wasted no time. His lips were all over Arianna's mouth and neck while she opened his pants and pulled out his cock. She stroked it until he lifted her onto the kitchen table, tore down her panties and thrust himself inside her.

Arianna's parents arrived early and almost walked in on them. Thankfully, Ti amo barked and alerted them. "Shit! Someone's here."

"Hello! It's Mom and Dad!"

"Oh God, it's my parents."

"You fix yourself and I'll go." Christiano painfully tucked himself in and headed to the door. "Ti amo, come to Daddy!" Ti amo ran over to Christiano. "You can come in now."

"We didn't think he'd bite us; we were more worried he'd run out." Jake extended his hand toward Ti amo. "Hey, Buddy."

Christiano tapped Ti amo on the head. "It's ok!"

Ti amo sniffed Jake's hand and then allowed Jake to pet him and in seconds they were friends.

"I baked some pies for dessert."

"Mmm, I love your pie." Christiano reached out his hands to take the pies from Alyssa.

"Where's Arianna?"

"She'll be right out."

"Can I help?"

"Nope, you two have a seat. I'll be right back."

Arianna picked up the vase of flowers as Christiano was on his way into the kitchen with the pies. "Everything ok?"

"Yes." Christiano kissed her on the cheek.

"I feel like we should be in trouble." Arianna giggled.

"But it was so worth it." He smiled.

"I love you, Chris."

"Love you too."

Josh and Monica let themselves in. Monica hugged Ti amo

who greeted them at the door. "How's my favorite furry friend?"

"Hey guys!"

Arianna hugged her brother and then Monica.

"Mom said she baked pies, so we stopped at the creamery and bought some ice cream."

"Oh yum! Thank you."

"Monica, Josh, thank you for coming." Christiano shook Josh's hand and then hugged Monica.

"Nice house, Chris, I'm so happy for you." She smiled.

Christiano looked over at Josh who was now greeting his parents. "I'm happy for you too."

"Guess we weren't meant to be together after all." Monica laughed.

"Not true. We are together as best friends."

The last guests to arrive were Giorgio and Daniel. Christiano knew his father considered Daniel an employee but to Christiano he was family. After Christiano reminded him that dinner at his home was no different than dinner at Giuseppe's Ristorante his father agreed to allow him to invite Daniel.

Christiano took a deep breath before opening the door. "Father, Daniel, come in."

His father stepped inside and looked around. "Why did you purchase such a small house?"

"It's just the two of us for now."

"It was only two of us at the mansion."

"Father, please, can we argue about..."

"I'm not arguing with you!"

169

"Fine. Come in and meet Arianna's family."

"Your father had me select your favorites." Daniel handed Christiano a case of wine.

"Thank you, Daniel, and thank you for coming tonight."

"You know, he does love you."

Christiano nodded. "I know."

Giorgio entered the room and Arianna and her family grew quiet as all the attention turned to the man who stood there with the cold stoic expression.

Christiano walked up behind his father. "This is my father, Giorgio and this is Daniel."

Arianna came over with her parents. "These are my parents, Jake and Alyssa."

Alyssa smiled. "Hello!"

Giorgio nodded.

Jake extended his hand. "Nice to meet you."

Giorgio shook his hand but didn't say anything.

Daniel waved. "Hello everyone. Pleasure to meet you."

Christiano looked as if he wanted to die from embarrassment. He poured his father and Daniel drinks, then swallowed down a shot.

Dinner was almost over. Arianna and Christiano tried to rush the evening along so that his father would be on his way. The tension was awful, and everyone was suffering from it.

Monica decided she would try to change the mood and

take the focus off Christiano and Arianna by talking about hers and Josh's wedding. "Arianna, I have something I'd like to ask you."

Arianna looked up. "Oh?"

"Since I don't have a sister of my own would you stand up for me at our wedding and be my maid of honor?"

Arianna covered her mouth and nodded. Monica came over to her and hugged her. "I'd be so honored."

Giorgio guzzled down the rest of his wine. He had no patience for sappy. "You know I find it quite amusing that you two are friends."

"Why is that?" Arianna looked at Giorgio.

Monica looked at Christiano in a panic.

"Usually one's ex does not befriend the..."

Josh looked at Monica. "Ex?"

"Father!"

Giorgio showed a hint of a smile cross his face. "Oh, they didn't know about you two?"

Josh threw his napkin down and walked out.

"Josh, wait!" Monica ran after him.

Christiano waited for Arianna to yell or cry but she simply looked away.

Monica caught up with Josh in the driveway. "Josh!"

"You know how I feel about him and all this time you never told me that you two..." He pulled open the car door.

Monica grabbed his arm. "That's why I never told you because of how you're acting right now!"

"So, you were just going to marry me and for the rest

of our lives it was going to be a secret between you and my brother-in-law!"

"Honestly, I don't see what difference it makes. It was a long time ago and we never dated."

"Great so you just spread your legs for him like a whore!"

Monica hauled off and smacked him across the face so hard that she left her fingerprints on his cheek. She pulled off her ring, threw it at him, and took off running down the driveway.

"Can I help you with anything?"

Arianna looked up at her mother. "Not unless you can undo the last few hours."

"I'm sorry, Dear."

"Poor Josh."

"What about you?"

"I don't know. I haven't even thought that far yet."

"Keep in mind that whatever happened with him and Monica was before you came along."

"I know but seeing as she is his best friend and also the woman who is marrying my brother, I think that they definitely should have mentioned it to us."

"Maybe they didn't mention it because it wasn't anything worth talking about." Alyssa picked up the pie and headed out of the kitchen.

Arianna let her mother's words sink in a moment before she picked up the coffee tray and followed.

Arianna no sooner closed the door after seeing her parents out when Christiano reached for her. "Ari!"

She pulled away. "I need time to think."

"Think?"

"Tonight, was mentally grueling; and now you and Monica. Yes, I need time to process this all."

"Monica and I never dated."

"No? Then what, a one-night stand?"

"Look, she was the first person I met after Lucia died and I needed someone. It was only supposed to be one night but…"

"But it wasn't, was it?"

"I've never cheated on you."

"No, but you lied to me."

"Lied? I've never lied to you."

"Do you still have feelings for her?"

"Feelings? Ari, I love you."

"Answer the question!"

"Monica is my best friend. I love her like a friend but, Ari, I am in love with you…not Monica. Never Monica."

Arianna stood watching Christiano, who looked as if he had lost his best friend. She wanted to forgive him, hug him, and make him feel better but she couldn't. Right now, she needed some time to settle things for herself before she could deal with him. "I'm going to bed."

"Ari, please!"

"I can't, Chris." Arianna walked away.

Christiano grabbed a bottle from the bar and headed out to the garden to smoke.

CHAPTER 26

Christiano woke up on the couch with a violent headache. He stumbled into the kitchen, pulled a bottle of water from the fridge, and grabbed some Tylenol from the closet. Ti amo trotted in behind him. "Hey, Buddy."

Ti amo sat and licked his hand. "Well, I guess I had better go try to get mommy to talk to me." Christiano headed down the hallway to the bedroom.

He panicked when she wasn't there. He pulled his phone from his pocket and texted.

Christiano: "You just gave up on us and left?"

Arianna: "I..."

Christiano looked down at Arianna's message, with that his phone rang.

"Ari, I can't believe you left me."

"You were passed out. I'm coming back. I only left to meet Josh. He's been texting for hours, so I finally decided to meet him for coffee."

"Oh...I'm sorry."

"Chris, Josh just walked in. We'll talk when I get home."

"Ok."

"No matter what, I love you."

Christiano smiled. *"I love you too."* He hung up and grabbed Ti amo. "Mommy still loves me."

"Hey!"

"Jeez, Ari, you look awful."

"Must run in the family."

Josh plopped down. "What are we going to do?"

"We?"

"Yeah. They lied to us. Now what?"

"Josh, I think we all need to find a way to work through this."

"So, you're going to forgive him?"

"While it would have been hard to hear from anyone, I definitely would have preferred to have heard it from Chris or Monica but it's too late for that now. What's done is done."

"But they lied to us."

"I said that to Chris last night. They never lied; they just didn't tell us."

"Ahh, so you're in lawyer mode now."

"Lawyer mode?"

"Yes, you're arguing their case."

"Fine. Maybe. All I know is that I don't want to lose the man I love because he failed to divulge something that he thought I was better off not knowing. To be honest, I wish I didn't know."

"I wish *they* never happened."

"Is it really worth losing Monica over?"

Christiano decided to call Monica and check up on her since he knew that Josh wasn't with her.

"*Hi.*"

"*How are you doing?*"

"I don't know. You?"

"Same. I'm waiting for Arianna to come home."

"Come home? She left last night?"

"No, although she went to bed and let it be known she wanted to be alone. But she's out now."

"At this hour?"

"I know, I thought she left me, but it turns out that she went to meet Josh."

"Oh."

"Yeah, she said he was texting her during the night, so she went to meet him."

"Do you think they'll ever forgive us?"

"I hope so because we didn't do anything wrong. It's not like we cheated on them or flat out lied. I mean, Ari never asked me about our relationship."

"Josh said things a few times, but it was his assumption that we never had sex and while I should have corrected him, I didn't."

"Why didn't you?"

"In hindsight, I guess I was afraid that he'd force me to sever ties with you."

"That would suck but, Monica, I'd understand."

"I wouldn't because that means that he doesn't trust me."

"No, it means that he is insecure."

"Whichever, I won't live like that."

"I understand."

"I hear the door. I'll call you later."

Josh was halfway through the living room when Monica walked in. "I wasn't sure you were ever coming back."

Josh dropped his keys down onto the coffee table as he sat. "You're the one that ran away."

"You called me a whore."

"I'm sorry. I shouldn't have."

Monica sat on the same couch but not right next to Josh. "I never meant to hurt you."

"I know, but you did. How many times did I say things and you remained silent?"

"I should have told you, but I was afraid that you'd make me end our friendship."

"Would you have if I asked you to?"

"Are you asking me to?"

"I don't know."

"You don't trust me?"

"Is there anything else that you conveniently never told me?"

"No, nothing."

"Do you love him?"

"As a friend, yes."

"Nothing more?"

Monica got up and began to pace. "You want complete honesty so here goes...When we first met, he was mess. He had just lost his fiancée and I didn't think I'd ever see him again, but I did. We talked more than anything else. We became quick friends and yes, we were friends with benefits. I had tried for more, but he always said no."

Josh stood up. "I've heard enough..."

"Sit, I'm not finished. Chris is my friend, only my friend. The night we had our first date I couldn't wait to go home and call him to tell him all about you. I was reluctant to date. Chris knew everything I'd been through, but he said you looked like a decent guy and he urged me to give you a chance. I'm so happy I listened to him because I found my soulmate. Josh, I love you."

Josh lifted his hand up toward Monica. "Come here."

Monica walked over to Josh and took his hand. "Josh…"

Josh yanked her down onto his lap and kissed her. "I love you too, Baby."

"Does this mean you forgive me?"

"I do, but this had better be the last time you keep something from me."

"I promise." She hugged Josh.

"Chris, I'm home."

"*I don't care what she signed or if we're married or not, Arianna is to be my sole beneficiary and that is final! Now, unless you want to look for another job, you will do as you're told and draw up the papers by the day's end.*"

Arianna walked up to the porch door and heard Christiano's conversation. "What's going on?"

Christiano shoved his phone into his pocket. "You're home."

"Is everything alright?"

"Oh, yeah, I was just taking care of business."

"I heard what you said."

Christiano looked at Arianna. "It's ok, I know you're mad, but I know you're not going to kill me for my money."

"Is someone going to kill you?"

Christiano shrugged. "It's always a possibility."

Arianna looked down. "I'm sorry I asked." She walked away.

Christiano followed her inside. "Ari, wait."

"Do you want a cup of coffee?"

"What I want is for us to talk."

"We've already established that you don't love her, and you've never cheated on me."

"Correct."

"So, is there anything else you should tell me, and I mean anything, because this is your one and only chance, Chris?"

"Do you want to know about every woman I've been with?"

"No, not unless they're having sex with my family members."

"At this time, she's the only one, but I reserve the right to speak up at a later date if someone else from my past pops up."

"Duly noted. Is there anything else?"

"I'm scared to death that I'm going to lose you."

Again, Arianna could see his sadness but this time she was ready to hold Christiano and forgive him. "Chris, you're not going to lose me. I just needed some time to process things."

Christiano pulled her tight. "You are my whole world."

Arianna kissed his chest. "And you're mine."

CHAPTER 27

"Excuse me, Arianna, there is someone waiting for you in the conference room."

Arianna looked at her calendar. "Who is it? I don't show any appointments until this afternoon."

Lynn waved for Arianna to come closer. "It was a last minute add."

Arianna stepped out into the hallway where Lynn was. "What's going on?"

Lynn pulled her halfway down the hall. "He said not to talk in your office."

Arianna's eyes opened wide and panic rushed through her. "Who is it?"

"He said he is a friend of Christiano."

"Ok. Thank you."

"Do you want me to come with you?"

"No, I'll be ok." At least she hoped she would.

Daniel paced as he waited for Arianna. He only hoped that what he had heard was a rumor.

Arianna panicked when she saw that it was Daniel. Her immediate thought was that something had happened to Christiano. "Is Christiano alright?"

"Yes. I'm sorry I didn't mean to upset you."

Arianna breathed a sigh of relief. "It's ok."

"Can we speak freely here?"

"I believe so. Daniel, what's going on?"

"I was afraid that your office may be bugged."

"My office?"

"Your boss is on payroll and..."

"You think..."

"I don't know what to think anymore."

"Which leads me back to what's going on?"

"I need your help."

"My help, not Christiano's?"

"He doesn't know I'm here and I hope it will remain that way."

"You want me to keep secrets from Christiano?"

"I don't think he's ready for what I am about to say."

"I know how much Christiano trusts you but, Daniel, I don't want to keep secrets from Christiano."

"If you think he is capable of handling this then you can tell him."

Arianna ran her hand across her face. "Alright."

"I was told that you're part of a team that's investigating the Bucati's. Is there any truth in that?"

"I was."

"Was?"

"I was approached shortly after my first encounter with Christiano and told that if I could help bring the family down that I'd be a shoe in for DA."

"I see."

"No, you don't. After a few dates I couldn't do it anymore. Daniel, I fell in love with him."

"I've spoken to people in all the different agencies. Arianna, Giorgio needs to be stopped."

"What about Christiano? As much as I despise his father if he goes down so will Christiano."

"I'm working on getting him immunity."

"Why are you doing this?"

"To protect Christiano. I promised his mother that I'd take care of him. I've already failed him once and I will not repeat my mistake."

"He loves you. I don't think he believes you've failed him."

"I could have warned him, but I was a coward."

"Warned him about what?"

"Giorgio is the one responsible for Lucia's death. He ordered her murder."

Arianna's blood ran cold. "Oh my God."

"I thought at the time he was going to pay her to leave Christiano. I didn't know that he was going to have her murdered."

"If Chris knew he was the one responsible he'd kill his father with his bare hands."

"I know and that's exactly why I never told him when I found out."

"Why tell me?"

"Because you're next."

Josh and Monica walked into the coffee shop and Josh came to a halt. "Why'd you stop?"

"I'll be outside." Josh turned and left.

It was then that Monica spotted Christiano paying for his coffee. She went after Josh. "Josh, wait up!"

"I knew it wouldn't be easy seeing him now that…"

Monica grabbed Josh's hand. "The past is the past."

"It just sickens me that he's had you."

"He's never had me like you do. Josh, I am so in love you."

"I love you too."

"Come on, let's go back and break the ice."

"Are you sure I can't break pretty boy's face?"

"JOSH!"

"Ok, I'll behave."

Because you are next kept resonating in Arianna's head, so much so, that she finally packed up her briefcase, canceled her appointments for the rest of the day and went home. She tore through some boxes to find the journal she initially began writing notes about Christiano. Once she found it, she started reading. It didn't seem that anything she had written wasn't already something Daniel didn't know. She did, however, have some recordings she made when Christiano spoke about business. If she gave these recordings to Daniel all it would do was implicate Christiano. Her mind was racing she closed the journal and was about to put it away when Ti amo started barking and then there was the sound of glass breaking. As she ran to see what was happening, she dropped the journal.

Once she made her way to the kitchen she peeked around the corner toward the door where Ti amo was barking. She could see glass on the floor and someone's arm working the lock. She ran to lock herself inside Christiano's panic room. She hoped that Ti amo would hold them off long enough for her to get inside. Once she was inside, she called Christiano.

Christiano was outside the coffee shop about to enter his car when Monica and Josh came walking back. He waved not knowing if he would get a wave back. It had been a week since hell broke loose and he had only spoken to Monica a few times when Josh was not home.

Monica waved. "Hey, Stranger!"

Christiano walked toward them. Typically, he would hug Monica, but for now it didn't seem like a good idea. "How's it going?"

"You know, it's going." Monica smiled and elbowed Josh.

Josh looked at Christiano. "Look, I don't like the fact that you're going to marry my sister and I despise the mere idea that you've…been with Monica, but they both mean a lot to me. For them I will make every effort to move forward and at the very least be amicable."

"Really, Josh!"

"It's ok, Monica, I'd rather he spoke the truth."

"Now, I'm going to grab some coffee." Josh stepped around Monica.

"Josh, it takes a big man to say what you did. I'm sorry you have so much hate for me. Hopefully, one day you won't."

Josh nodded before walking away.

"I'll be right in." Monica looked back toward Christiano. "Thank you, Chris."

"Sure."

"I know…"

"Hang on its Arianna calling." Christiano answered. *"Ari, can I…"*

"Chris, someone's in the house."

"You're home from work?"

"Yes. Help me."

It was as if ice ran through Christiano's veins. *"I'm on my way. Don't hang up."*

Monica could see something was terribly wrong. "What is it?"

"Call 9-1-1, send them to my house!" Christiano hopped in his car and sped away leaving Monica in a frenzy.

Arianna listened to Christiano as he gave her instructions on how to load his gun should she need it. Her hands were shaking. She knew someone was in the house because the alarm chimed when the door opened.

"They're inside. Chris, I hear gunshots."

"I'm almost home. The police should be there any minute."

"I'm so sorry I didn't turn on the alarm. I was so distracted." Distracted that someone was going to kill her and well, here they were. So much for being warned.

"Shhh, I know you're scared but you're going to be alright. There's no chance of anyone getting into that room."

"Oh God, I don't hear Ti amo barking. Chris, what if…"

"Don't go there. The police…"

Arianna looked down at her phone. The battery died. She dropped it to the floor.

Christiano's heart sunk when the phone went dead, he called back several times but no answer. As he approached the house it was like everything was in slow motion. Two police cars were in the driveway. He had to force his way inside. Once he was inside, he saw a body on the floor, one of his men in a chair holding a bloody towel against his shoulder, and the other talking to a police officer. He finally made his way down the hall with the police in tow. Seeing the door intact and Ti amo sitting guard in front of it calmed his nerves a bit but until he held Arianna in his arms he couldn't breathe.

"Ti amo, good boy." He greeted the dog as he motioned for him to step aside. He entered the code and pulled the door open. "Ari!"

Arianna was curled up in the corner with her arms wrapped around her knees, holding Christiano's gun. "I thought I was going to die."

Christiano dropped to his knees and held her. "Oh, Angel, I've got you. You're ok."

Ti amo came over and rubbed his snout against her cheek. Arianna pet his head. "You were such a good boy, Ti amo."

"Ma'am, do you require medical assistance?"

Arianna looked up at the officer. "No, I'm ok."

"Come on, let's get you out of here."

CHAPTER 28

D aniel dropped the newspaper down onto Giorgio's desk. "It looks as if your attempt to take out Arianna was thwarted by your son's security team."

Giorgio glanced at the newspaper headlines *Home Invasion or Retaliation?* before dropping it into the wastebasket. "Ironic isn't it."

"Sir, have you considered bringing her into the fold. A woman in her position has many resources."

"She doesn't have it in her. That's what draws my son in, it's her good nature. He sees his mother in these women and then becomes putty in their hands."

"What if Christiano can't survive without her? He barely made it through last time. Is that something you're willing to accept?"

"I know that you think you know what is best for *my* son. As his father, I am certain he will channel his anger as he did the last time and become stronger. Hurt and anger are fuel for people like us." Giorgio smiled.

"You and I both know that Christiano only killed the three men who murdered Lucia after you handed him the gun and practically pulled the trigger yourself. The poor boy was in a fragile emotional state, under the influence of medication, and you still needed to push his buttons until he finally complied. Do you honestly think that killing Arianna will cause him to suddenly transform into the man you've always wished for?"

"My son made me proud that day. I waited his entire life to see him make his first kill. My blood runs through his veins and I will be damned if he will follow the path of a weak man. He is a Bucati!"

"May I enter?" Rex stood in Giorgio's doorway.

"Come in."

Daniel stepped back. "I will let you two speak."

"Wait, you should hear this too."

Daniel stopped. "What is it?"

"Speak, Rex!"

"It looks like my informant found our mole."

Daniel's palms began to sweat. He knew that Giorgio wouldn't waste any time blowing his head off.

"Well, who is it? Don't just stand there staring at me!"

"Pino."

Daniel blinked. He pushed his hands into his pockets and tried to breathe. "Pino?"

Giorgio sat back in his chair. "Bring him to me now!"

"He's gone missing it seems."

"Missing or into hiding?"

"He didn't show up to his last meeting with the feds I was told."

"I want him found!"

"I'll never tire of waking up to those gorgeous green eyes."

"Not even when I'm old and gray?"

"Nope. Never."

"You know what I'll never tire of?" Christiano rolled Arianna over and in one fell swoop thrust himself inside her. "This. When I'm inside you I have hope."

"Hope?"

Christiano kissed Arianna. He didn't want to talk, he wanted to make love to her.

Once Arianna's lips were free, she asked again. "Honey, is everything ok?"

Christiano tried to kiss Arianna again to silence her but she moved her head. "Can't we talk later?"

"I'm worried about you."

Christiano pulled out and leaned back on his heels. "Hope…that one day we can be free."

"Of your father?"

"Yes. I know I'll never be free of all the terrible things I've done but…"

"Chris, you can walk away whenever you want."

"No, you don't understand, it isn't that easy."

Arianna sat up. "Isn't it. We can start over anywhere you want."

"My father won't let me go."

"Is it your father or are you afraid?" Arianna reached out her hand. "I'll follow you anywhere."

"For myself, no. I know that at any given time someone could put a bullet in me and I'm ok with that. What I'm afraid of is that he will find us and blame you."

"So, then we don't let him find us."

"My father has men everywhere just waiting to take someone out. Until he's gone, I'll never be free."

Daniel hid up the street until he saw Arianna's limo pull away. He knew that Christiano wasn't allowing her to go anywhere alone until they found out if it was a home invasion or some sort of retaliation. As he lifted his hand to ring the bell Christiano opened the door. "Daniel, what are you doing here?"

"We need to talk."

"Come in."

Daniel walked inside and gave Christiano a nod. "I stopped by to tell you that they found the mole." Daniel continued walking until he reached the panic room.

Christiano nodded. "Really who?"

"Pino."

"How did you find out?" Christiano opened the door.

"Why don't you get ready to leave and I'll explain in the car."

Christiano followed Daniel inside and closed the door. "What the hell is going on?"

"We need to talk, and I had to make sure that it was secure."

"You think my house is bugged?"

"Possibly and it isn't a chance I'm willing to take."

Christiano could see how serious Daniel looked. "Ok."

Daniel reached inside his suit jacket, pulled out an envelope and handed it to Christiano. "This is yours."

Christiano took the envelope, pulled out the papers, and began reading. "Where did this come from?"

"Your mother asked me to hold it until it was time…and its time, Christiano."

"First off, where did all this money come from, and second, time for what?"

"Your father grew his empire with your mother's money. Not that your father was a pauper by any means, but it is your mother who was the wealthy one. She was born into money. Your great-grandfather Mario Angelino had many small villas and inns across Italy. It was his dream to own a hotel which he eventually did, and so the story goes."

"I never knew any of that."

"As far as Giorgio is concerned it is his business. You see after your parents married your father had some shady dealings and came into a bundle of cash. After a while he finally strong armed your mother into practically begging her sisters to allow him to buy them out of the business. He paid them a hefty sum and honestly, they were happy to break the ties with Giorgio. Tina couldn't stand him."

"Wait, you know my mother's sisters?"

"I grew up with them. Your mother and I met in grade school."

"So, that's why you've always taken such good care of me." Christiano smiled.

"Your mother loved you so much. She always said, you made it all worth it."

"All? What do you mean?"

"Your parents had an arranged marriage."

"No, that can't be. Mom always seemed so happy...until she grew ill."

"She was happy because she had you."

"At first she was devastated that she had to leave the man she loved but after a while she got used to your father. He treated her well, and I can honestly say, he was truly devastated when she left us."

"I can't believe this. The thought of losing Ari..."

"Your mother hoped and prayed every night that one day you'd find the love that she once had."

191

Christiano looked at Daniel and he could see unshed tears. "You're him?"

Daniel nodded. "It was never my intention to tell you."

Christiano stood up. "Mom brought you to work for us so that she could have her cake and eat it too?" Now Christiano almost felt bad for his father.

"No. She hired a few of us from our hometown. Your father needed loyal men."

"Real loyal sleeping with his wife and all." Christiano looked at Daniel with disgust.

"Your mother was faithful to your father until a few months before she died. Do you remember the last trip we took to see your aunts?"

Christiano sat and thought back to that visit. "Yes, of course."

"Your father sent me along to take care of you and your mother because she was in such a fragile state. We never intended for anything to happen; I swear, but it did. Your mother, she begged me. She said she always dreamed of being in my arms. It was her dying wish. It was more emotional than physical."

"Didn't it eat at you day after day to see her with my father?"

"Yes, I tried to get over her, but you know how those marriages ended. As much as it hurt me to stay though, it afforded me to remain in her life. After we lost her, you were the only thing that got me through. I'd look into your eyes and I would see your mother's kindness and her smile when you'd smile." Daniel wiped his eyes.

Christiano cleared his throat. "I'm sorry that I didn't know sooner."

"It wouldn't have made a difference. She's gone. I can only hope that she's the first person I see when I cross those pearly gates."

Christiano reached over and placed his hand onto Daniel's shoulder. "I'm sure she will be."

Daniel's phone rang. "It's your father."

Arianna was greeted by security inside and outside her office. "How are you doing?"

"Hey, I'm sorry I didn't call you back last night."

"It's ok. I understand."

"How's my big cranky brother?"

"He's ok."

"And you?"

"Are we ok?"

"Do I wish you never had sex with Chris...yes, but you did. I can't change it and I also can't avoid you like an ex, since you're going to marry my brother."

"I'm sorry that you have to be made to feel that way, but I'm not sorry that Chris and I became friends. We helped each other through a lot. He was so broken when I met him and now that he's with you he's whole." Monica smiled.

"Thank you for saying that. I'm hoping once the shock wears off and time passes it will be a faint memory."

"Good because I really love Josh and I want all of us to get along."

"I want that too."

Christiano sat thinking about his mother and how she was forced to live her life with a man she didn't love; alongside the man she loved and couldn't have.

"I told him I came to bring you up to date on Pino and drive you into work."

"Daniel, you told me about the money but why now?"

"Because it's time for you to get a fresh start."

"You want me to use this money to get away from my father?"

"Yes."

"No amount of money can buy family and if I take Arianna and start over what happens to her family…and you?"

"I'm begging you to go. Take Arianna and start over. You won't have to hide forever. I promise."

"What's that supposed to mean?"

"I have a plan."

"To take my father down. What about me, you, and the rest of the men?"

"The men will scatter. You will be taken care of, I promise. I have your back."

"What about you?"

"If I'm still standing, I'll figure it out."

Christiano stood up. "Take this. You go, you start over. Let me take care of you for a change." He handed Daniel the envelope.

Daniel shook his head. "I can't. I promised my sweet, Bella that I would care for you. I let her down one too many times. Please go. Take Arianna and go…before it's too late."

"Too late?"

"It's just a figure of speech."

"No. It wasn't. Did my father have anything to do with

the intruder? Was he trying to scare Arianna into leaving me...or worse?"

Daniel's silence spoke volumes. Christiano opened the door and took off running.

Daniel set out to follow Christiano but stopped when he spotted Arianna's journal peeking out from under the bed. He picked it up wondering why she left it lying around for Christiano to see. He'd have to discuss that with her later. Right now, he needed to stop Christiano.

CHAPTER 29

Christiano came flying into the house in a rage. "FATHER! FATHER! WHERE ARE YOU?"

Rex came running into the foyer. "What's going on?"

"Where is he?"

Rex tried to grab Christiano's arm to cool him down but Christiano slammed Rex face first into the wall. "Get the hell out of my sight before I kill you too!"

Rex backed down but he was not going to retreat. He followed Christiano as he went room to room until he found his father in his library.

"WAS IT YOU?"

Giorgio calmly looked up from his desk as if he hadn't heard Christiano's voice billowing throughout the house. "Sit!"

Christiano balled his hands into fists and stomped over to where his father was sitting. "Did you send that man to invade my home?"

Giorgio dropped his pen and stood up. "Is that what the police think?"

"No. It's what I think."

"Would you like to know what I think? I think that it's a pity that man was killed before he took out your pathetic whore of a fiancée!"

Christiano shoved his father into the bookcase. Giorgio laughed. Christiano pulled his gun. "I. HATE. YOU. I. HATE..."

A gunshot rung out and Christiano staggered back before dropping to the floor.

Giorgio looked up and Rex was standing there laughing. "Brat! You should have taught him to respect you like I do."

Giorgio pulled his gun and without a word shot Rex in the head. He dropped to Christiano's side. "Son! Son!"

Daniel heard the gunshots and he died a thousand deaths. What he didn't expect was to see Giorgio still standing and Christiano bleeding to death on the floor. "Oh my God!" Daniel dialed 9-1-1. *"Send an ambulance for a gunshot wound. I'm not sure if he's breathing."*

Giorgio looked down at the blood on his hands. "Help him! He isn't breathing."

Daniel started CPR. Within minutes the ambulance arrived. Daniel and Giorgio stood there helpless as they watched the team work to revive Christiano.

Daniel called Steve on the way to the hospital and asked him to tell Arianna and let her know a car was waiting downstairs for her. Steve took a deep breath before knocking on Arianna's door. It wasn't the kind of news anyone ever wanted to hear.

"Arianna, I need to tell you something."

Arianna's world spun. "It's about Chris isn't it?"

Steve nodded. "There's a car waiting to take you to him."

"Where is he? What's happened?" She could barely get the words out through the tears.

"He was shot."

"Oh my God! Is he…dead?"

"No, but his condition is grave. I'm sorry."

197

Arianna kept nodding her head as she grabbed her phone and purse. She wiped her eyes. "Thank you for letting me know." She was in shock.

"Do you want me to come with you?"

"No." She pressed the elevator button, it opened, and she was gone.

Steve knew Arianna had her brother listed as her emergency contact, so he went into his office to look up Josh's number. He knew Arianna would need someone to be by her side.

Daniel got them to the hospital and then one of the orderlies led them to a private bathroom where they could wash off the blood. After that they just sat silently waiting on pins and needles for word on Christiano's condition. Minutes seemed like hours.

Arianna came flying into the waiting room. "Where is he?"

Daniel got up and walked over to her. "Surgery."

"What happened?"

Giorgio sat staring. "Rex shot him."

"Daniel, how could you let this happen? It's your job to take care of him!" Arianna started pounding her fists on Daniel's chest. "Where were you?"

Daniel grabbed her and held her tight. "I'm so sorry. I was parking the car."

The police came into the waiting room to talk to Giorgio and Daniel. "So, what happened?"

"My son and I were discussing business when my employee, Rex…"

"The dead guy?"

"Yes. He shot my son in the back and then aimed at me. I pulled my gun and fired."

"Let me get this straight, he walked in shot your son and then you shot him?"

Giorgio nodded. Daniel looked at the police. "That's what happened. I was on my way down the hallway when I saw Rex approach the library, pull his gun and shoot. Then he pointed the gun at Mr. Bucati, who shot back. Rex dropped to the floor, and I called 9-1-1."

"Alright. Don't leave town."

Arianna paced as she prayed. Daniel walked over. "Can I get you anything?"

"You know I spoke to those people you asked about and got the wheels rolling. Guess it won't matter much now."

"It's not over yet."

"I have this awful feeling it is."

"ARI!" Josh grabbed Arianna and hugged her.

Monica stood next to him crying. Arianna reached over and hugged her. "We didn't have enough time."

"Is he gone?" Josh wasn't a fan of his, but he certainly didn't want to see him dead.

"They haven't told us anything since we arrived, except that he is in surgery."

"So, there's hope." Monica wiped her eyes.

"We had a disagreement. I never should have left him."

"Ari…"

"If he survives this, I am going to make certain that we leave this life and start over."

Arianna bolted from her seat when she saw a man in scrubs walking toward her.

"Is someone here from the Bucati family?"

"I am." Arianna stepped in front of the doctor.

"You are not family. I am his Father."

"Come with me." He waved Giorgio on.

Arianna looked at the doctor. "I'm his wife!"

All eyes turned to Arianna. "She's lying." Giorgio grunted.

"We were married in Italy."

The doctor held up his hands. "Stop! You can both come with me."

Arianna followed the doctor and Giorgio through the doors until the doctor stopped in front of a curtain.

"We did all we could, but he lost too much blood. I'm sorry. I'll leave you to say your goodbyes."

"No…no…oh, God, no." Arianna pulled the curtain back. Christiano had tape and needles sticking out of his arms and chest. She took his hand. "How will I go on without you? You made me promise never to leave you, and now you've left me."

Giorgio stood frozen. He knew that if he said goodbye then he would be accepting the fact that his son was gone. He turned and walked back to the waiting room.

"How is he?"

Giorgio looked up at Daniel and shook his head. "You were more of a father to him than I was. You should be in there." Giorgio left the waiting area.

Daniel wrapped his arms around Arianna. "I'm so sorry. So sorry."

"We really did get married in Italy. He was waiting until his father accepted me…"

"If I was a minute sooner…"

"He's finally free now."

"Excuse me, are you his wife?"

"Yes."

"Here are his personal effects."

Arianna took his wallet, watch and phone. As she put them into her purse Daniel heard something drop. He reached down. "I haven't seen this since Bella died."

Arianna looked up. "He always kept it with him."

"May I?"

Arianna nodded. Daniel opened it. He expected to find the picture of Bella on one side and Christiano on the other, but instead Christiano had replaced his picture with Arianna's. "How am I going to live without him?"

"It's time to go now."

Arianna looked at the nurses and then Daniel. "We can do this…together." Daniel nodded. He knew he had to be strong for Arianna.

Daniel leaned down and kissed Christiano on his forehead. "Goodbye, Kid. Tell your mother I'll always love her."

Arianna could barely see through the tears. She placed

her cheek against his and whispered in his ear. "I will love you forever. Wait for me."

She turned to Daniel and he wrapped his arm around her. She gave Christiano one last glance and blew him a kiss.

By the time they got back to the waiting room Daniel was practically carrying Arianna. Josh ran to her side. "Ari…"

Daniel nodded. "He's gone."

Monica dropped down into her seat and kept shaking her head. "No. He can't be gone."

Josh walked Arianna over to where Monica was sitting. "Why don't I drive us all to mom and dad's house."

"No, I want to go home. I need to walk Ti amo."

"Ari, I can go by the house and…"

"I need to be home."

"Ok, we can take you there."

"Daniel, will you come with us?"

"I need to check on Giorgio. Perhaps I can come by later?"

"You're always welcome." Arianna hugged him.

"You call me if you need anything."

Arianna nodded. Josh held her hand and wrapped the other arm around Monica's waist. "Let's get you home.

CHAPTER 30

Arianna cried herself to sleep with Ti amo beside her. Josh and Monica stayed until their parents arrived. Josh insisted she not be left alone.

"Ari, you need to eat."

"I can't."

"Honey, the next few days will be horrible, I won't lie, but we will get through this together."

"Easy for you to say when your husband is still alive. Mine is DEAD!" Arianna rolled over and put the pillow over her head as she burst into tears.

Alyssa rubbed Arianna's back while she cried. Her heart broke for her daughter.

Monica woke up, opened her eyes, and then closed them.

Josh didn't say anything he just held her and kissed her cheek.

"I was hoping it was a bad dream."

"Nope."

"I still don't believe it. After all he went through...he finally found a woman he'd allow to love him. It's not fair."

"Arianna didn't give him much of a choice did she."

"I remember how they looked at each other that first time they met."

"I want you to know that I am not happy he's gone."

"I never thought you would be."

"I feel guilty that I pretty much wished him dead because…"

"Shhh! Josh, we all do those things. You were upset. I get it."

"I want you to know that I'm here for you. Whatever you need."

"Thank you."

Daniel was barely surviving on an hour sleep and three espressos. He felt as if his heart had been ripped out. Saving Christiano may no longer be his goal but saving Arianna from the wrath of Giorgio certainly was. He was surprised to see Giorgio sitting in his office looking stoic as usual. One would never know that his son was murdered in the room down the hall less than twenty-four hours ago. Daniel had stopped back at the house on his way home from the hospital and Giorgio was conducting overseas business and waved him off. His behavior was disheartening at the least.

"Daniel, have you something to say?"

"I'm sorry, Sir, I was sadly recalling the events of last night."

"Yes, I did as well, and I've concluded that if my son wasn't so much like his mother, that he'd still be with us."

"Well, I am quite certain that he is with Bella now."

"I suppose." Giorgio looked back down.

Monica knocked on Arianna's door. "Ari, can I come in?" Monica didn't wait for a reply. She opened the door, came in and climbed on the bed.

"I can't believe I'm never going to see him again."

"Thank you for making his last days his happiest ones."

"I'm sorry we got married without you."

"Me too. Do you want to talk about it?"

"We stayed at this beautiful villa. I loved it so much that he bought it for me as a wedding gift. We planned to go back and…"

"Oh, Ari." Monica squeezed her hand. "We don't have to talk about it."

"Chris was so afraid that if we waited that something would happen. He told me that Lucia was killed right before their wedding."

"She was."

"He asked me to marry him after dinner that first night. The garden was filled with roses and lots of twinkling lights. He looked so nervous and adorable." Arianna looked down at her ring. "We ordered custom wedding bands. I wonder if they have a return policy."

"Arianna! You can wear them on a chain."

"It wasn't more than an hour after I'd agreed to marry him that a van pulled up the driveway and started unloading wedding gowns. I felt like a princess. I found a simple yet elegant dress. It was an off the shoulder white satin ball gown. I didn't want a veil, so the hairdresser gave me an up do and added some small white roses to my hair. They matched Chris' boutonniere. My bouquet had roses and sweet peas."

"Did you take any pictures?"

"We planned to go back and meet with the photographer.

My dress is there with my bouquet. Chris was having them preserved for me."

"Maybe when you're ready Josh and I can take you back."

"I think I'm done talking for now." Arianna rolled over and closed her eyes.

"I thought I saw someone out here."

Daniel looked up. "Crazy but I hoped that maybe I'd still be able to smell his tobacco."

"You know that Christiano and I didn't get along too well, but I really am sorry he's gone."

"You were just looking out for the women you love. I get it."

"So, what's big man Bucati up to today?"

"Business as usual. You'd never know he watched his son get murdered last night."

"Why do you work for him? I mean you seem like a nice guy."

"I took the job because I wanted to be close to Christiano's mother and then after she died, I stayed because I promised Bella I'd look after him. Too bad I didn't do a good enough job."

"Who knew one of his own men would turn on him."

"I couldn't save Christiano but I'm going to make damn certain that your sister never has to worry about a thing."

"Worry? About what? Is my sister in danger?"

"I didn't mean to upset you. I am aware of how much trouble Giorgio can cause."

"Aside from seeing my sister at Christiano's services he shouldn't have any reason to be in contact with her."

"Christiano left everything he had to your sister which means she is now business partners with Giorgio."

"The hell she is. I won't have my sister mixed up in anything that has to do with the Bucati name."

"When your sister is up to it, she can decide how she wants to proceed." Daniel got up and walked inside.

"Can I see Arianna?"

Alyssa and Monica both pointed down the hall. "She won't leave the bedroom."

"I'll see what I can do."

Arianna was sitting up in the bed with Ti amo sprawled across Christiano's side of the bed. She was holding Christiano's pillow.

Daniel knocked.

"Come in."

"How are you holding up?"

"I'm not. What about you?"

"Same."

"I did what you said. We were so close to being free."

"Well, we're going to keep working on that. If Giorgio is in the picture, we are all at risk."

"You think he still wants me dead?"

"Christiano left you everything. His homes, cars, money, and his half of Villa Resorts and Hotels. He inherited his mother's half when she died."

"If I'm to inherit half then would that give me access to see the books?"

"I know what you're getting at, but it sounds way too dangerous."

"I don't have anything else to live for, besides Christiano told me it is easier to hate then to feel pain."

207

CHAPTER 31

Three months later…

"You're sure you're ready?"

Arianna nodded her head. "I've been waiting all day."

"Ok, let's take a look."

Arianna smiled. "She's beautiful."

"She?"

"Since I found out I was pregnant I've just had this feeling it's a girl."

"Do you want to know?"

Arianna nodded. "Please."

"You're right you're definitely having a girl."

Arianna rubbed her belly. "I can't wait to meet you, Bella."

"It looks as though you won't have to wait as long as you first thought."

"What do you mean? Is something wrong?"

"No, not at all. In fact, she's perfect for a third trimester baby."

"But how? How could I not know?"

"You've been under so much stress and my guess is that your loss of appetite made up for the baby's weight."

"I don't look that pregnant, what if she didn't get enough…"

"Calm down. The bloodwork is fine. I would like you to try to eat more often even if it is small portions."

"Oh, I'll eat. She's all I have left of my husband. I don't want anything to happen to her."

"I will see you next month. If you have any questions or concerns call me."

"Thank you, Doctor." Arianna looked down at the sonogram pictures. "I wish your daddy was here to see these."

"Mom, Dad, you home?"

"We're in the kitchen."

Arianna came into the kitchen and her parents both looked at her like she had three heads. "Are you alright?"

Her mother walked over to her. "Maybe you should sit down."

"I'm fine."

"What's going on because we haven't seen you look this happy in months."

"Mom, Dad, I'm pregnant."

"Pregnant!"

"Yes." Arianna held up the sonogram picture.

Her mother looked at it. "Yes, that definitely is a baby." Her mother hugged her.

"Whose baby is it?"

"It's Chris' baby."

"Oh, so you're already more than three months. Is that why you waited to tell us?"

"No, I just found out. I'm in my third trimester already."

"This sounds fishy. Are you sure?"

"Dad, I'm sure. Here, look." She handed him the sonogram picture.

"I'm so excited. I'm going to be a grandmother."

"I came straight here so please don't tell anyone until I get to tell Josh."

"We're here for you and this little one." Jake patted Arianna on the back.

"Oh, it's a girl. Her name is Bella."

Alyssa looked at Jake and smiled. "Are you hungry? Would Bella like grandma to cook something for her mommy?"

"That would be great mom. I need to make sure I eat from now on."

"Your mother has that covered; she loves to cook."

"Daniel, have you seen Arianna recently?"

"Not since last week. Why?"

"I just hung up with Carlo, he said she was at the medical building on Fifth and it seems as if she could be pregnant."

"Pregnant?"

"I thought maybe you knew and were keeping quiet."

"No. My loyalty lies with you." Daniel almost choked on that lie.

"I think you should pay her a visit and find out what's going on."

"I will head over once I take care of the Statler account."

"Good. Because if there's a chance that she is carrying *my* grandchild I have a right to know."

"Yes, Sir. I will contact you as soon I speak with her." Daniel couldn't contain his excitement at the thought that Arianna could be carrying Christiano's baby.

"PREGNANT! HOW?"

"Really, do I need to draw you a picture." Arianna laughed.

Monica squealed and hugged Arianna. "I'm going to be an aunt."

"To a niece."

"It's a girl?"

Arianna held her belly. "Her name is Bella."

"HELLOOOO!"

Arianna and Monica looked at Josh like he was crashing their party. "Josh, you're like a wet blanket." Monica shook her head.

"Who have you been sleeping with?"

"It's Chris' baby."

"But it's been months."

"Yes, and I'm quite pregnant. The doctor said it happens."

Josh hugged Arianna. "I'm really happy for you, Sis."

It had been a long day. Arianna stumbled into the kitchen grabbed a bottle of water and gasped. She pulled open the door. "You scared the hell out of me."

"I'm sorry."

"Come in."

"Come out."

Arianna smiled. She knew that sitting in the garden reminded Daniel of Christiano. "Ok. You win."

"I'm here on official business."

"I was going to call you tonight."

"Really? Why?"

"I'm having Chris' baby. It's a girl and I've already started calling her Bella."

Daniel's eyes swelled with tears. He got up and hugged Arianna. "Bella would be honored to know her granddaughter was named after her."

"Daniel, I want you to be part of Bella's life. There's so much you can tell her about her father."

"I'd like that. Thank you."

"Now, what official business brings you here?"

"I was sent to find out if you were pregnant."

"Is he having me followed?"

"Honestly, I don't know if it was intentional or coincidental, but Carlo spotted you coming out of the medical building and told Giorgio."

"This *was* a good day." Arianna rolled her eyes.

"Hey, don't allow him to ruin this for you."

"How can I not? The last thing I want is for him to lay claim to my baby." Arianna held her belly.

"That's not something you're going to have to worry about. I promise."

"You can't promise that."

"Our 'new friends' are days away from…"

"They've been promising us any day for the last two months."

"Bringing down someone like him takes time."

"We gave them so much information. I hoped that would be enough to get this over with."

"Well, if that baby comes before they take care of him, then I will."

"Daniel!"

"Because of him we lost Christiano, we will not lose his daughter."

Giorgio hung up with Daniel and poured himself a drink to celebrate. He raised his glass. "To my newest heir."

"Sir, you have a call."

"Who is it?"

"Mrs. Bucati."

Giorgio swallowed down the rest of his drink. "Thank you, Lyle. You can go."

"Yes, Sir."

Giorgio sat and picked up the phone. "Hello."

"I'm calling to let you know…"

"That you are expecting my son's baby?"

"Thanks to your henchman my husband is dead which means that this baby is mine."

Giorgio's blood started to boil. He stood. "Regardless of what you think that child is MY son's and I will make certain that she is raised as a Bucati!"

"Over my dead body!"

"As you wish." Giorgio ended the call.

Daniel rushed back inside when he saw Arianna's expression change through the window. "What did he say?"

"He demanded to raise my baby as a Bucati and when I said it would be over my dead body he replied with, 'as you wish' and hung up."

"Look, right now you and your baby are safe. He won't jeopardize his grandchild."

"How can you be so sure when you know how much he despises me?"

"Yes, and once your child is born, I agree, that he will kill you."

"I think it's time I used some of that blood money."

"For what? You can't exactly pay a hitman to kill him!"

"No but my brother had this military friend years ago that he would threaten my boyfriends with…"

"Threaten how?"

"He would tell my boyfriends that if they didn't treat me right that all he had to do was make one call."

"Ari, involving another criminal…"

"No, he's a good guy."

"A good guy who kills people." Daniel laughed.

"I should have thought about him sooner. I have to call Josh."

Daniel wasn't sure who this real-life superhero was but he sure as hell hoped that he was the answer to their prayers.

CHAPTER 32

Arianna and Josh were picked up in a big black SUV the next night. Josh's friend was very secretive about everything. He told them he couldn't risk being recognized so they'd have to come to him.

"You doing ok, Sis?"

"Yes. Thank you for doing this."

"Stop thanking me." Josh turned in his seat and took Arianna's hand. "You're my sister and that is my niece you are carrying. I am not going to let big man Bucati bring you any more pain, not now, not ever."

"I love you."

"I love you too."

Arianna looked at the window. "I've never seen a window that you couldn't see through. Almost creepy in a way."

"I'm sure it's for our protection and I'd venture to say that they are bulletproof as well."

"Where do you think we're going?"

"Probably somewhere close to an airport. He'll fly in and out. I'm telling you this guy is a genius ghost on steroids." Josh laughed.

"I wish I could remember him."

"The only time you would have met him was at our boot camp graduation."

"I was too busy checking out all the hot guys to pay attention to your geek friend."

"I'm not into guys but he's far from a geek. Hell, he could be a model."

"Is he married?"

Josh rolled his eyes. "Really!"

Arianna laughed. "Gotcha!"

"Jerk!"

Two hours passed before Arianna and Josh were led down a damp dark hallway into a small room that had a table and four chairs. "You can have a seat. I will let him know you're here."

Arianna looked around. "Josh, if he wasn't a trusted friend, I'd be afraid he brought us here to kill us!"

"Perhaps I did."

Arianna's eyes grew wide. "That's him behind me isn't it?"

Josh laughed. "Yup!"

Arianna turned around. "I'm sorry."

"You're good."

Josh walked over and extended his hand. "Thank you for helping us."

Arianna stood there silently as she gave the gorgeous geek with beautiful blue eyes and devilish smile a once over.

"I hope I can."

Josh elbowed his sister. "Ari!"

Arianna shook her head. "I'm sorry. I checked out for a minute." She gave them a quick smile.

"That's the smile I remember."

"You remember me?"

"Photographic memory." He pointed to his head.

"Impressive."

"Have a seat and let's talk."

"So, a…" Arianna looked at the sexy geek.

"I'm crushed you don't even remember my name." He laughed. "It's Beck."

"Is that your first name or your last name?"

"Ari, Beck is a busy man…"

Beck held up his hand to Josh. "Beck McQueen, at your service." Beck extended his hand.

"You already know my name and…who my husband was." Arianna wiped a stray tear. "I'm sorry. You'd think I was all cried out by now."

"No worries. Did you bring everything I asked for?"

Arianna nodded and then pulled a thick folder from her tote bag. "That's everything."

Beck skimmed the files. "Those alphabet agencies have been working on this for how long?"

"I've been working with them for over three months, but Daniel began months before."

Beck shook his head. "What a joke." He stood up.

Arianna sprung up and grabbed his arm. "WAIT!"

Beck looked down at her hand and then back up. "I know I'm irresistible, but I have a plane to catch."

Arianna's face dropped and she let go. "I'm sorry we wasted your time." She blinked away another tear.

Beck lifted his hand and placed it onto Arianna's shoulder. "I came here to help you."

"But you're leaving?"

"Yes, I'm leaving so that I can get this taken care of before my next mission."

"Oh! I thought you were leaving because…"

"I pretty much single handedly took down the Grimaldi and Notelli families last year. Bucati is going to be like a walk in the park."

Josh shook Beck's hand. "I owe you."

"Owe!" Arianna reached into her purse and pulled out a wad of cash. "Start with this and then…"

Beck waved her off. "Friends don't owe friends. Now you go home and take care of that little one." Beck kissed her on the forehead.

"Josh, Semper Fi!"

"Semper Fi!"

Daniel was waiting in the garden when Arianna came home. "I somehow figured I'd find you out here."

"How did it go?"

"He seemed confident that he could help. Said that he took down the Grimaldi and No…"

"Notelli?" Daniel's eyes widened.

"That's it. Have you heard of them?"

"So, he was wearing a cape."

"Huh?"

"Those families were way more powerful than Bucati's organization. Damn, Ari, we may finally be free." Daniel hugged Arianna.

"I wish Chris was still here."

"Whoa!"

Arianna smiled. "You felt that?"

"I think she's going to be a soccer player."

"She can be anything she wants to be, and I will love and support her."

"As any loving mother should."

Josh snuck into bed thinking that Monica was asleep, but she wasn't. She rolled over. "How'd it go?"

"He said he'd take care of it."

"You don't sound convinced."

"Let's say I'm trying to be cautiously optimistic."

"It would be nice to be able to go to sleep at night and not have to worry."

"Yeah."

"Too bad Chris was never able to experience that."

"No, but at least his daughter will be able to."

"We will all make sure she does." Monica pulled Josh close and kissed him.

"LYLE!"

"Yes, Mr. Bucati."

"Pull up the car."

"Yes, Sir."

Giorgio pocketed his phone.

"Are you going out?"

"Yes, I've decided to pay my son's whore a visit."

"Try to remember that she's carrying your granddaughter."

"That's the only reason she is still breathing, and I want her to know that."

Daniel felt sick to his stomach. "Would you like me to come with you?"

"No." Giorgio walked out.

Daniel reached for his gun and for a split second almost ended it right then and there. In fact, he would have except he promised Arianna he would wait.

Arianna poured herself her one allotted cup of coffee for the day and sat to read her book on parenting.

Ti amo barked at the door. Arianna looked over at the security camera and saw Giorgio getting out of his car.

She got up and prepared for a confrontation. Once the doorbell rang, she took a deep breath and then opened it.

Giorgio's eyes went straight to her belly before looking her in the eye. "Arianna."

Ti amo stood at her side. "What are you doing here?"

"I want to discuss my granddaughter."

"There is nothing to discuss!"

"Then you can listen…"

"Goodbye." Arianna swung the door to close it, but Giorgio stuck his foot inside before it closed.

"My granddaughter will be raised as a Bucati, by me, in my home. You see her mother is going to have a tragic accident following her birth and being an orphan, her Papa will take full custody."

"No court would ever give you custody!"

"Oh, don't be so naïve you know how the court system works. Anyone can be bought."

"I'm a lawyer and I have an iron clad will leaving full custody to my brother and his soon-to-be wife; along with enough money for them to raise Bella so that she will never want for anything."

Giorgio let out a laugh. "You're not as stupid as you look, however, once you're out of the picture your plans for my granddaughter won't matter."

Once he removed his foot, Arianna slammed the door, ran to the bathroom, and vomited.

CHAPTER 33

"**S**urprise!"

Arianna gasped as she looked around at all her family and friends. "Oh, Guys!"

Josh and Monica ran over to her. Josh kissed her on the cheek. "Hey, Sis!"

Monica draped a mommy-to-be sash over her belly and then rubbed it. "We can't wait to meet you baby, Bella."

Alyssa hugged her daughter. "I know you're not in a party mood lately, but we have to celebrate this precious little bundle you're carrying."

"Thank you, Mom."

"Selfie time!" Jake pulled Arianna close and snapped.

"Dad, I look awful."

"You look beautiful and one day Bella is going to want to see what she looked like in your belly."

Arianna smiled. "Ok, take two!"

Josh handed Arianna a piece of cake and sat. "How are you holding up?"

"I'm hanging in there."

"It's been a week since we met with Beck. I'm sure we'll hear something soon."

Arianna nodded. "We still have time." She rubbed her belly.

"I will kill that bastard myself before I allow him anywhere near Bella."

"Ari, your phone sounds like its exploding." Monica laughed.

Arianna took the phone, swiped the screen, and burst into tears.

Josh's phone vibrated in his pocket. "Oh, my, God!"

"Josh!" Monica put her hand on his shoulder.

"Turn on the TV."

Monica ran over to the bar. "Turn on the TV!"

The bartender clicked on the TV. "What channel?"

"Josh, what…holy shit!"

Arianna stood with her family and friends watching the news. "I wish I knew if Daniel was alright."

Monica rubbed her back. "Did you text him?"

"Damn, when my man said he brought down the house, he meant it."

"Josh, I don't know how I'll ever be able to thank him."

"He'd say to forget you ever met him and never speak his name." Josh kissed Arianna's head.

"Ari, I think it might be best if you stay with us tonight."

"Why, Dad?"

"We don't know if there will be any repercussions…"

"And the press may also hound you, Dear."

"Mom, Dad, I appreciate your concern, but I've been alone for months now and I need to take care of myself."

"Will you at least promise that you'll call us if you need us."

"Scout's honor." Arianna held up her three fingers.

Arianna pulled into her garage, got out, turned around, and Daniel was standing there. She grabbed her belly. "My God, you scared me!"

"Close the door."

Arianna leaned over and pushed the button to close the door. "You ok?"

Once the door closed Daniel practically ran over to Arianna and hugged her. "It's finally over!"

"I was so worried about you. We watched them raid the house and the offices on the TV."

"Some guy grabbed me before I made my way inside the house. He said Josh told him if anything happened to me that his sister would be devastated."

Arianna smiled. "I would be. Aside from this precious baby you're my only link to Chris."

"Well, then I guess sitting in that van for six hours was worth it."

"Now what?"

"I have to meet with the authorities tomorrow. They didn't arrest me so that's a plus." Daniel laughed.

"Daniel, do you think that maybe after Bella is born you could take me to your hometown to meet Chris' aunts?"

"I will take you and Miss Bella anywhere in the world once I'm cleared to leave the city."

"We are so lucky to have you in our lives."

"Ditto."

Arianna rolled over, picked up her phone and started to scroll through texts. Next, she opened her web browser to check the weather and that is when she saw the headlines. *Giorgio Bucati Found Dead.*

Arianna reached for her phone. *"Josh, have you seen the news?"*

"No, we're still in bed. What's going on?"

"Giorgio was found dead in his jail cell."

"There is a God."

"Josh, is everything ok?"

Josh nodded. "Someone offed big man Bucati."

Monica sprung up. "Karma is a bitch."

"I'll let you go. I need to pee." Arianna laughed.

"What was that?"

"Huh?"

"It's been so long since I've heard you laugh."

"Hopefully, I can begin to heal now."

"You know who to call if you need help."

"Thank you."

Arianna heard Ti amo barking at the front door. "Ti amo! Is someone at the door? Of course, I don't expect you to answer me, but you look so cute when I talk to you." Arianna opened the door. "Can I help you?"

"Arianna Bucati?"

"Who are you?"

The man pulled a badge and ID from his suit pocket. "Agent Kian."

"I'm Arianna Bucati."

"I was asked to hand deliver this to you."

Arianna took the envelope. "Thank you." She closed the door and walked over to the couch. Ti amo climbed up next to her. "Ti amo, I'm honestly afraid to find out what's inside this envelope." Ti amo barked and then pressed his snout up against her hand. "Alright, I'll open it."

Arianna opened the envelope and pulled out the documents. Inside was documentation regarding the acceptance of Christiano's plea deal. Daniel told her he had set up a plea for Christiano as well. She tossed it onto the coffee table. "I don't need those papers to prove that your daddy was a good man." Ti amo barked. She gave him a pat on the head and a kiss. "You know, Ti amo, for the first time in a long time, I think everything is going to be ok.

EPILOGUE

Three months later…

"I cannot believe that baby slept the whole flight over." Daniel smiled at Bella.

"She's perfect in every way." Arianna smiled.

"Perfect or not, I still think you should have taken a few more weeks to rest."

"I'm fine, Daniel. Truth is, I needed a change of scenery. With Bella coming early and all, I spent way too much time thinking while I sat in the NICU."

The limo pulled up the driveway. Arianna looked at the beautiful villa Christiano bought her as a wedding gift. It seemed like that was a lifetime ago. "Ari."

"Sorry, I was lost in thought."

"Why don't you head inside and get Bella's room settled and I'll sit with her."

"In case I forget to tell you, thank you for coming with us."

"Papa Daniel was honored that you invited him to escort you two lovely ladies." Daniel smiled.

"No matter how grim of a day, you can always make me smile." Arianna ran her finger across Bella's locket. "Mommy will be right back."

Arianna lifted her hand to knock for the housekeeper to let her in when she caught a whiff of tobacco. It had been months since she'd smelled tobacco. Funny how a smell she once hated brought her comfort. She walked around the back of the villa to the garden passing the beautiful roses along the way. She leaned forward, closed her eyes, and inhaled the rose's fragrance as she remembered her wedding.

When she opened her eyes, she froze, two sparkling green eyes stared into hers. Time seemed to stand still. She couldn't speak and her hands began to tremble.

"I can explain later, but right now I just really want to hold you in my arms and never let you go."

His voice made him seem real, but he couldn't be, the man she loved was gone. Arianna blinked, took a step back and shook her head.

It wasn't until he reached out his hand and touched her that she believed he was real. "But…"

Christiano wrapped his arms around her and held her tight. "I love you so much."

Arianna pulled back and looked up at him. "How could you make me think you were dead all this time…do you have any idea what I've been through?"

"I didn't know what happened. I woke up in the hospital handcuffed to a bed. They told me I had been shot and as far as anyone knew I was dead. Nobody asked me if I wanted to play dead, Ari, they forced me. I tried to bribe anyone I could to get me a phone or get a message to you, but they wouldn't budge. When I was strong enough, they sent me to a safe house in the woods of Montana under heavy guard. They kept telling me it was for our safety. Then some guy raised hell and they accepted my plea deal. I thought I was finally going home when we boarded the plane, but we ended up in Rome. Seems that I needed to deal with legal matters here as well. They finally let me leave the compound I was at under house arrest three days ago."

"Why didn't you call me then?"

"I called Daniel first because…I was afraid that maybe you'd moved on or…"

Arianna shook her head. "Never. You took my heart and soul with you when you left me."

"Daniel told me you already had plans to come here, so I decided to wait and tell you in person."

"I can't believe he didn't tell me. Wait until I see him."

"He didn't come with you?"

"I left him in the car."

"He came all this way with you, and you didn't think to invite him in?"

"I will in a minute. First, I need to do this." Arianna wrapped her arms around Christiano and kissed him.

Daniel sat impatiently in the limo waiting for Arianna and Christiano to come out from the garden. He couldn't wait to see Christiano again but was in no rush for the tongue lashing he expected Arianna to give him.

"Oh, Bella, here comes your mommy and daddy and they're holding hands." Daniel opened the door and stepped out.

Christiano picked up his pace until he reached Daniel. "I've missed you." Christiano grabbed Daniel and hugged him.

Daniel didn't want to let him go. "I told you I had your back, Kid."

Christiano and Daniel separated and Christiano

immediately focused on Arianna who was standing there holding Bella. Arianna smiled as she walked toward Christiano.

Christiano looked down at the baby and then up at Arianna. "Bella Christine, meet your daddy."

Christiano had tears rolling down his cheeks. He ran his hand through his hair. "Why didn't you tell me?"

"You were dead until two minutes ago."

"I meant before I was...dead."

"I was in my third trimester before I found out. Then this little princess showed up a month early."

Christiano ran his finger across the locket. "Ma-Ma's locket."

"They gave it to me at the hospital the day you..." Arianna cleared her throat. "I wore it until I took her home from the hospital.

"Can I...hold her?"

Arianna nodded. "Here you go, Daddy."

Christiano looked down at his daughter. "I can't believe you made her while I was...I'm so sorry you had to suffer because of..."

"Chris, if this is the end result, then it was all worth it." Arianna kissed Bella.

Christiano wrapped his free arm around Arianna's waist and pulled her against him. "When you promised you'd never leave me, you took it to heart."

"A promise is a promise."

"I love you both with all my heart and soul."

"We love you more."

The End

OTHER BOOKS

Made in the USA
Middletown, DE
18 March 2022